ne

"Jarod, I couldn't possibly—"

"You couldn't possibly refuse," he interrupted, turning on the full force of his charm. "Look, Sabrina, this is the perfect situation. You've just decided to stay in Tulsa, and you don't have a job. I have to have a manager for my store very soon, and I have no idea where to get one." He smiled. "If you say no, I don't know what I'll do. I'll lose thousands of dollars because the store won't open on time; I'll hire worthless, lazy employees who'll steal me blind; I'll buy all the wrong stock, and the customers will never come back a second time; I'll . . ."

She began to laugh. "You'll get along just fine. You won't have to worry about a thing."

She had to tell him no. An unequivocal no. How could she even consider working with him, being with him all the time? If she were alone with him, if he kissed her again, if he touched her the way he had last night, she knew they would end up making love.

D1048128

Dear Reader:

A writer's first book often portrays her homeland. And why not? In school we were all taught to write about what we know best. For five of Silhouette's most innovative writers, Oklahoma is more than home: Oklahoma is the blood that runs in their veins. Ada Steward, author of two Special Editions about this pioneer state, writes that Oklahoma is "a land and people still untamed beneath their veneer of civilization."

Starting with February 1986, Silhouette Special Edition is featuring the AMERICAN TRIBUTE—a tribute to America, where romance has never been so good. For six consecutive months, one out of every six Special Editions is an episode in the AMERICAN TRIBUTE, a portrait of the lives of six women, all from Oklahoma. AMERICAN TRIBUTE features some of your favorite authors—Ada Steward, Jeanne Stephens, Gena Dalton, Elaine Camp and Renee Roszel. You'll know the AMERICAN TRIBUTE by its patriotic stripe under the Silhouette Special Edition border.

AMERICAN TRIBUTE—six women, six stories.

AMERICAN TRIBUTE—one of the reasons Silhouette Special Edition is just that—special.

The Editors at Silhouette Books

★ AMERICAN ★ TRIBUTE ★

GENA DALTON
Cherokee Fire

Silhouette Special Edition

Published by Silhouette Books New York

America's Publisher of Contemporary Romance

For Harry and Helen,
with love and appreciation.

SILHOUETTE BOOKS
300 East 42nd St., New York, N.Y.   10017

Copyright © 1986 by Genell Dellin

ISBN: 0-373-09307-1

First Silhouette Books printing May 1986

America's Publisher of Contemporary Romance

Printed in the U.S.A.

Where a man's dreams count for more than his parentage . . .

GENA DALTON

is a wife and mother as well as a writer, but her interests don't stop there. She is fascinated by Ozark-Appalachian folk culture, does tole painting, gardens and is interested in horses.

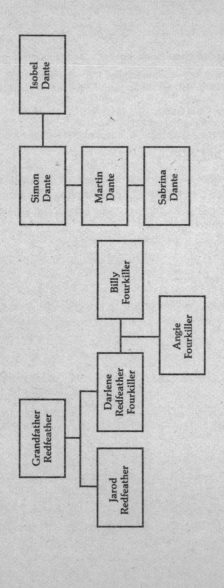

Chapter One

The copper sunlight filtered through the leaves of Mohawk Park's big oaks without losing any of its heat, so when Sabrina wandered into a deeper shade she stopped in the coolness for a minute. She glanced back the way she had come. The glint of the polished grill on her mother's Mercedes was winking at her from the parking area. I ought to go back to the car and turn on the air conditioner, she thought. I ought to go home.

"Would you like to join us?"

Startled that someone was close enough to speak to her so quietly, she whirled.

Sabrina was standing almost in the middle of a camp set up for the three days of the annual Tulsa powwow; two women were working at a cooking fire just on the other side of her big shade tree. The one who had spoken was watching her with kindly eyes, the other didn't look up from her stirring.

"No...no, thank you."

She smiled at the woman, drawn to her by the natural friendliness in her face, then moved away. I don't belong here, she thought, turning back toward her car; she was wandering around intruding on people's privacy without even knowing it.

She stepped over a protruding root so she could circle the tall canvas tepee of the camp next door. A teenage boy dressed only in a breechclout, moccasins and several layers of carefully applied paint was just outside it, standing with one foot on a bench and the other on the picnic table. He was fastening fluffy leg ornaments topped with tiny bells around his calves.

"Hey, Wayne, bring me my headband," he yelled.

Another boy stuck his head out of a nearby camper-topped pickup truck. "No way," he answered with a wide grin. "Not till you pay what you owe me." He revved the truck's motor and pantomined putting it into gear as if he were going to drive away. The first boy leaped off the table and ran to him, shouting good-humored threats.

Another reason to leave, she thought, watching them. Everybody in the whole park seemed to know everyone else, except for her. She had no idea how to approach any of them with questions about her Cherokee heritage, and she didn't feel one bit closer to her father's memory here than she did at home. She should have listened to Martin.

She crossed the asphalt road, walking faster because the heat that the June sun had stored in its surface was seeping up through the thin soles of her sandals. This had been a ridiculous idea in the first place. She'd go straight back to her mother's house and spend the rest of the day by the pool.

But the enormous green-and-white-striped awning of the arts and crafts tent stood between her and the car. When she reached it she tried to pretend that it wasn't there, but her merchandising instincts were too strong. She hesitated, then decided that the Indian craft work was probably too good to pass up. If she could find a new item for the department store chain to carry, then this afternoon wouldn't be a complete waste.

She lifted the flap and went in. Several people, mostly whites with cameras, were drifting along the aisles in the welcome dimness. She joined them.

There was an enormous variety of goods on the long tables, and she moved slowly, examining them carefully. Surely she could find some jewelry, shawls or baskets for the new One of a Kind Boutique at Harwell and Neel's.

She stopped in front of a table covered with paintings displayed on small wooden stands. An easel stood on one, holding a painting much larger than the rest. They were strikingly well-done, all of them, but the big one caught at her heart. It portrayed a mother carrying a child through the snow, an armed soldier on horseback between them and some other vague figures on foot. A narrow, hand-lettered placard beneath it proclaimed the title: *Triumphal Journey*.

A girl of about sixteen with huge brown eyes sat behind the table in a folding lawn chair; an ancient man in a matching chair was beside her. Sabrina glanced at the signature on the painting and back to the girl.

"Are you Angie Fourkiller?"

"Yes."

"And you called this *Triumphal Journey* because your people survived their Trail of Tears?"

Surprise lit the girl's eyes. "That's right."

The old man cleared his throat, a discordant raspy sound too loud to come from his wizened body. But when he spoke his voice was very soft. "Some did," he said. "Some died."

"I know, Grandpa," Angie said. "But if *any* of the Cherokee lived, we were triumphant." Her tone was patient but her expressive face said that they'd exchanged those words before.

She turned to Sabrina to cut off the familiar conversation. "You're only the second one that understood my title. Most people say the same thing Grandpa does. They think I should've called it *Sorrowful Journey* or something like that."

"But the triumph is there. It's easy to see. It's in the way the woman carries herself and the child." Sabrina continued to study the painting. "You're a good artist, Angie."

Angie's smile was shy but radiant. "Thank you."

Sabrina returned it. "I'm Sabrina Dante," she said, holding out her hand. Angie shook it firmly, then indicated her grandfather with a small, respectful gesture. "This is my Grandpa, Ridge Redfeather." The old man nodded, but he made no move to take Sabrina's hand.

"It's nice to meet you," Angie said. Then her eyes darted to a spot behind Sabrina and she grinned mischievously. "Here comes Jarod. I can't wait to tell him!"

Sabrina turned. There was only one man coming toward them, but there could have been a dozen and her eyes would have found this one. And would have clung to him.

He was tall and she could see that under the silky shirt his chest and shoulders were heavily muscled. But it was the way he carried himself that held her attention. He moved with a confidence, a sureness, that was beyond arrogance. Every line of his body carried a natural sense of its own power that was mesmerizing.

He has it all together, she thought suddenly, with a little pang of envy. *He knows what he wants and he's going after it.*

She didn't move or take her eyes off him. His long legs swung from the hips in a cowboy's deliberate, rolling walk, yet there was a smoothness in his gait, an underlying flow in every step that spoke of his Indian heritage just as clearly as did his high cheekbones and the proud chiseled straightness of his nose.

His face wasn't conventionally handsome, she decided then, too fascinated to realize that she was staring at him. It was too strong and too rugged for that. It was magnificent.

The dark coals of his eyes met hers for a super-charged second, then they were smiling at Angie.

"Jarod," she called to him. "Guess what! You're not the only one who's so smart. Sabrina understood the title of *Triumphal Journey*, too!"

"Sabrina?"

His voice was low-pitched and resonant, as rich as the burgundy color of the Western-style shirt he wore.

"This is Sabrina Dante," Angie said. "Sabrina, this is my uncle, Jarod Redfeather."

His eyes were even darker than she'd thought. They met hers easily and she glimpsed the serenity she'd sensed in him earlier. Then they were glinting with a mischief like that in Angie's grin.

They didn't leave Sabrina's as he inclined his head toward Angie's painting. "So you knew what she meant," he said. "Not bad. Not bad at all for somebody who isn't even Indian."

"But I am!" Sabrina blurted. "I'm Indian, too."

He watched her eyes deepen from sky-blue into the color of smoke with the passion in her tone. Contradictory as well as beautiful, he thought. All cool and sleek on the outside and full of fire on the inside.

"Another one of Oklahoma's blue-eyed one-sixteenth Cherokees, huh?" he teased.

"How did you know one-sixteenth?" she demanded. "How did you know that?"

"I can just tell," he said, looking her over with the leisurely air of a professor examining a new specimen. "I can tell by..."

"Jarod, you stop that!" Angie interrupted indignantly, eager to protect the dignity of her new acquaintance. She turned to Sabrina. "Sabrina, don't you listen to him, don't believe a word he tells you."

His smile was incredible. It was a grin, really, a crooked grin that changed his face from magnificent to marvelous and gave him the air of a little boy who was very sure of his ability to charm.

"I couldn't *really* tell," he admitted, still holding her eyes with his. "But you know how it is. Everybody in Oklahoma claims to be at least one-sixteenth Indian of some tribe or other, and it's usually Cherokee."

"And they're always descended from a Cherokee princess," Angie chimed in.

Sabrina was lost in his smile. "I don't know anything about a princess among my ancestors, but I do know my tribe is Cherokee. I just found out about it a couple of days ago." She dropped her eyes and glanced around her with a little shrug. "That's...that's sort of why I came."

"To find out what it's like to be Indian?"

"Yes."

"Well, then," he said, as if that one word had appointed him host for the occasion, "I'll show you around. We'll have some fry bread and watch the fancy dancing exhibition."

She hesitated, but he didn't seem to notice. He turned to speak to Grandfather Ridge and Angie smiled at her, completely shy again.

"It was nice to meet you," she said softly.

"You, too, Angie."

Jarod began moving with Sabrina toward the exit, leaving the dim coolness of the tent before she had time to think. She was more aware of his big hand hovering protectively at the small of her back than she was of exactly where they were.

Once outside, they walked slowly, the sunshine holding them together in a shimmering cocoon. He guided her through the noisy crowd that seemed to be growing by the minute and stopped at a concession stand, its sign proclaiming Indian Fry Bread. They waited in companionable silence to be served and she glanced up at him, astonished with herself for being there. She certainly wasn't accustomed to running around powwows, or anyplace else for that matter, with a man she had just met; but somehow, at this moment, she couldn't imagine walking away from him.

He handed her the fragrant bread, hot from the deep fryer. "There you are," he said. "Your first lesson in Indian education. Any Cherokee worthy of the name eats fry bread."

She gasped in dismay. "It's too much!" she exclaimed. "I can't eat all of this!"

"Wait till you taste it. You'll change your mind," he promised. "Bite into it or tear off a piece, whichever," he said. "Then I'll pour some honey onto it for you."

She followed instructions and juggled the sweet, warm food from one hand to the other as he led her away from the booth.

"Okay, that takes care of food," he said briskly. "Now for the dancing."

"You mean this is the *only* food that's traditionally Cherokee?" she teased. "That part of my education's finished?"

"Only for now," he said, with that grin that melted her bones. "You're not ready for connuche yet, but we'll get to that."

She stood still, smiling back at him, forgetting to listen to what he was saying.

Finally the words came through. "Dennis Bluecorn's the lead fancy dancer; let's go sit down and watch him. The drum sounds like he's about ready to start." She willed her feet to move.

The drumbeat grew louder as they crossed the narrow road and moved into the space between the sets of bleachers. It was steady and compelling; it began to work its way into her head as he led her to a camp chair at the very edge of the dancing ground, one of several with Redfeather stenciled across the back.

She settled into it and waited while he shook hands with a man behind them and waved to someone across the circle. Then the high-pitched, solemn sound of the singers began and Jarod was sitting beside her, bending his head to hers to tell her about the song.

A man's melodious voice boomed over the music through a public-address system. He hadn't finished the words "Dennis Bluecorn" when the dancer's feet hit the packed earth in front of him, carrying him into the circle with an energy so powerful that it seemed to be from another world.

Sabrina drew in her breath and held it, mesmerized by the whirling force in front of them, completely caught up in the vivid colors of the feathers and paints the man wore, spellbound by the relentless, rhythmic stroking of his moccasins against the earth.

"He's . . . he's wonderful," she whispered.

Jarod spoke as softly as she had, but his answer rang in her ears as if he'd shouted. "I knew you'd like this."

She shivered a little, although it wasn't chilly. The sun was just beginning to slip behind the trees and the air was as close and hot as ever. He *had* known that, she thought. It was as if he knew *her*. As if he'd known her for a long, long time.

The dancer was coming around the circle, drawing nearer and nearer to them, and his movements were slowing from the frenetic burst of his dramatic entrance. He was bending his whole body sinuously forward and then back with the deliberate beat of the drum, stretching so that his head feathers could brush the ground behind him. He was an erotic image of manhood, clad only in a breechclout and the bright orange and red feathers, the light glinting off the muscles rippling under his warm bronze skin.

It made her even more acutely aware of Jarod so close beside her, of his arm touching hers. She could feel the heat of his body through the silk of his sleeve.

She looked up to find his eyes on her.

The taste of the honey on her lips, the sound of the drum and the song in her ears and the sight of the primitive movements in front of her were enough to make Sabrina solely a creature of her senses. But they were not what was doing this to her.

It was the dark eyes gazing into hers, the touch of his arm, the fragrance of leather and soap and a faint cologne. All the sensations that were Jarod Redfeather were filling her with feelings more powerful than all the other sense impressions put together.

She tore her eyes away and fastened them on the dancer again. He finished his circuit and passed the entrance to the circle where he'd first appeared; as he did so other dancers began to pour into the dancing ground behind him.

She and Jarod sat without speaking, watching the enchanting flood of color and movement that was the perfect accompaniment to the beat of the drum and the high, minor tones of the song. They hardly moved for half an hour, until the arena was filled with constantly undulating bodies. Then Jarod touched her hand.

"Let's go get something to drink. This will be going on for a while."

He held her hand as they slipped out through the crowd and kept it until they'd bought the soft drinks. His fingers brushed hers again as he handed her the paper cup, and then, as they stood facing each other sipping at the icy liquid, it seemed strange to her that they were no longer touching.

"What dances come after this?" she asked, surprised to hear a breathlessness in her voice.

"The brush dance and then the gourd dance. That's the one Ridge and I will dance in."

"Oh. Then you'll have to go and change soon."

Her eyes were that smoky color again; and as they took in his jeans and shirt he could almost feel them on his skin. He could almost feel her *hands* on his skin.

He smiled and shook his head, resisting the urge to reach out and lift the shining black wing of her hair away from the curve of her neck.

"I'm dressed to dance," he said. "Gourd dance costumes aren't quite as flashy as the fancy dancers'."

"Well, I'm disappointed!" she teased, amazing herself by actually putting her fantasy into words. "I'd be happy to wait while you go and change into feathers and a breechclout like Dennis Bluecorn's." She matched his smile. "After all, Jarod, that *is* the accepted image of an Indian dancer."

His smile deepened into that grin again. "You've seen too many movies, Sabrina. Hollywood doesn't know a thing about Indians."

"Are you sure?"

"Positive."

The insane, teasing words hung in the air between them, their meaning unimportant, their tone everything. It was warm and close, the spoofing sound of two friends who knew each other well.

His eyes held hers and the sensual awareness she'd had of him during the dancing returned a thousand times stronger. She knew he was feeling it, too; it was vibrating between them on every beat of the powerful drum.

Then the drum stopped, and so did the singing. She dropped her eyes to the cup in her hand. She had to get control of herself and of this situation.

"Okay, let's go see this brush dance," she suggested. "Didn't you promise to educate me?"

"I did," he affirmed. "And I will. I don't intend for you to miss a single attraction of your first powwow."

But even though they started to, they didn't go back to their seats. They stopped at the end of the wooden bleachers as if they had an unspoken agreement to stay separate from the rest of the crowd. They stood there to finish their drinks and watch the first groups of dancers leave and others arrive.

Three or four men together, then several women in another group moved from the folding chairs nearest the arena to the long wooden benches that encircled it, while adjusting their fringed shawls and sashes. A few at a time, they stood and began to dance, coming from each of the four directions, inching gracefully inside the very edge of the dancing ground. They were all moving closer to the drum, but the segregation never changed.

"Don't they ever dance together?" Sabrina asked. "The men and the women, I mean."

Jarod didn't answer for a moment and she glanced up at him. The glint of mischief was in his eyes.

"Sometimes. Come here and I'll show you."

He took her hand and led her to a little clearing in the trees just behind the announcer's stand, out of reach of the arena's tall lights.

"This is the way they dance together," he murmured, taking her into his arms for a few intricate steps. His closeness tightened her chest; it made her breathing light and brought it into perfect rhythm with the pulsing beat of the drum.

Then he was holding her away from him, gesturing for her to stand still while he began dancing in a circle around her. She watched him, fascinated. The fiery wine color of his shirt caught the faint light left in the darkening evening, and his skin was burnished with the same deep glow.

His movements were sure and sensual, slower than those of the head fancy dancer they'd watched earlier, but just as enticingly erotic. He caught her up in them entirely, their rhythm flowing naturally with the insistent beat of the drum. She was aware of nothing but him and the music and the night; he was a lodestone that drew all of them together and used them to pervade her depths.

By the time the music finally stopped she was dizzy with him. He whirled to a halt and held out one hand; she grasped it tightly, feeling as if she would fall without his support. She couldn't take her eyes from his face, this stranger with the inexplicable hold over her.

Finally, to try to break his spell, she forced herself to speak. "What...what dance was that?" she asked. "What's its name?"

"I don't know," he drawled, his face perfectly solemn. "I just made it up."

She stared at him incredulously for the space of half a minute, then she began to smile and they broke into wonderful laughter.

It feels so good, she thought. So good to laugh.

With a little shock she realized that this was the first time she'd laughed since she'd gotten the news of her father's death. Maybe it *would* get better, she thought. Maybe she *was* going to heal after all.

But she knew when she looked up into Jarod's eyes again that even before that sadness she'd never laughed in quite this way.

Because she'd never known a man quite like this. He was so different, so good, so full of some earthy basic warmth that was entirely new to her. A sudden surge of hope flowed into her. The whole world wasn't lonely and perhaps she could learn not to be.

"Not all our dances have names," he was saying in his soft, rich voice, using his professorial tone once more. "But we always dance for the really important things like rain...and a good harvest...and for the chance to see a beautiful lady again."

She stared into his compelling eyes. She nodded slowly.

"We might even go dancing again," he suggested.

"Only if you promise to wear feathers."

He grinned. "I promise."

"Where *is* the next powwow? Maybe there's one at the Cherokee reservation—you know, down by Tahlequah."

"There aren't any reservations in Oklahoma! The whole *state* is a reservation!" He was horrified. "Sabrina, where did you grow up?"

"In Tulsa."

He shook his head ruefully. "I can't believe it." Then the teasing grin lit his face again. "We haven't been down on the reservation at all; we've been surrounding you all your life and you didn't even know it."

"What do you mean 'we'? Remember I'm an Indian, too!"

"Not until you get a little education, you're not. Your ignorance is abominable."

She smiled. He sounded exactly like the professor she used to have for business law.

"Your first assignment is to go with me to Tahlequah, all right. How about tomorrow night?"

"You must think my case is urgent."

Her tone was unabashedly flirtatious, her lips full and soft, pouting a little at him. He fought the urge to kiss her. He couldn't. If he did, he wouldn't be able to stop.

Instead, he said, "Not just urgent. It's almost terminal. It's downright embarrassing for you to go around telling people that you're Cherokee, even if it *is* only one-sixteenth. Tomorrow night."

She laughed. "All right."

"I'll pick you up around five. It's a long drive."

She nodded mutely and they stood very still, looking into each other's eyes. That same wordless communication was alive between them—they couldn't stand there any longer without touching again and both of them knew it.

"I'll need your address," he said at last. His voice was a little bit hoarse, as if he hadn't spoken for a long time.

She reached into her bag and found one of her business cards and a pen. "I'm staying at my mother's right now," she murmured, holding the slim purse flat to support the card as she scribbled on the back. "This is her address."

She finished and handed it to him, her whole world contracting in that instant to the intensity in his eyes and the rough, warm feel of his fingers against hers.

"I'll see you tomorrow, Sabrina," he said softly.

Then he was gone into the trees.

The night wind picked up and rustled the leaves. She listened to it and stared in the direction Jarod had disappeared, realizing for the first time that it had grown completely dark.

She reached out to touch the trunk of a tree as if she needed something solid to hold on to. What had she done? She'd made a date with a man she didn't even know. A man totally unlike the ones she *had* known.

She began running her hand over the sycamore's rough bark as she heard the drum begin again and the swell of the song rise with it. Those primal sounds pulsed into her veins and with them a knowledge from a sure, inexplicable instinct: she'd finally met a man who could unleash all the riotous emotions that had always simmered beneath her surface.

A little chill of fear chased through her. She might not be ready for that, after all.

Chapter Two

The doorbell rang almost as soon as the massive oak panels swung closed, and Sabrina shifted the bag of books in her arms so she could see her watch. It surely couldn't be Jarod yet—hadn't he said five o'clock? She went back to the door and opened it to find her brother, Martin.

"Are you the new maid?" he greeted her, smiling. "No, can't be. The uniform is far too chic."

"Since when have *you* ever noticed chic?" she retorted, smiling back and stepping aside to welcome him in. "You've worn the very same kind of suit every day of your whole life," she teased. "You think that ordering up clones of your basic outfit in different colors and fabrics every season is the way the whole world lives."

He laughed. "Not fair, not fair at all." He reached to take the bag from her as they crossed the foyer and headed down the hall toward the spacious sun room.

"Good grief, Sabrina, this is heavy! What've you bought now?"

"Books. I had a few minutes so I ran down to Steve's to get a history of Oklahoma and a Cherokee history. I found a couple of other things, too." She took the bag from him and started spreading out the books on the long library table behind the sofa.

He glanced at the titles and then away. He crossed the room restlessly and dropped into a deep chintz-covered armchair.

"Are you still off on that Indian tangent? I thought you forgot all about that when we decided not to go to the powwow."

"*You* decided not to go. I went."

His eyes flicked to hers, surprised. "You did? Well? Was I right?"

"At first I thought you were. But then I talked to a few people and they made me feel welcome. After that it wasn't boring at all. I really enjoyed the dancing." Her stomach contracted at the memory of Jarod's arms around her and the dance he'd made up just for her.

"Well, that's good," Martin said. He wasn't truly interested, though. He was staring out at the huge trees on the lawn that sloped away from the house, his mind on something else.

She walked around the end of the table and sat on the couch across from him. "You know, Martin, after watching the Indians last night and talking with some of them, it's interesting to think about Dad's being one-quarter Cherokee."

His eyes flicked to hers.

"And about our being a sixteenth."

"Perhaps, but we're still the same people we were before we knew we had any Indian blood."

"Yes, but they seem so different from us somehow."

"Well, Dad wasn't very close to his roots, Indian or not. He was one to live entirely in the present...at least as far as we knew."

Their eyes held. The room became very quiet. Sabrina felt tears prick at her eyes again. She and Martin had never been tremendously close—there was a nine year difference in age and a world of difference in their interests—but at that moment she knew they were thinking identical thoughts, having identical regrets.

She dropped her eyes and closed them against the pain. Had it only been a week since that awful evening after the funeral when she and Martin had gone through their father's papers? It seemed more like a month to her.

They'd shared the same emotions that night, too, she remembered. After the last of the friends and relatives had gone and their mother had disappeared into her room, the two of them had wandered restlessly through the house bound together by a sinking sense of loss and by that horrid feeling of wanting to find their father, of needing somehow to try one more time to be close to him. Finally the yearning had drawn them into his study and into looking through the documents in his desk as if they might find a message from him there.

And so they'd stumbled onto the papers he'd always kept private. Private. The word slashed at her. Private was the perfect word for Simon Dante.

She looked up at Martin, her eyes brimming with unshed tears. "You know, those records of Cherokee blood we found among his papers—" she paused to stop the trembling in her lips "—his mother's tribal enrollment and the receipts for the contributions he'd made to the Kee-Too-Wah tribe...Martin, that's probably only one of dozens of secrets he kept from us. We never really knew Dad at all."

"I know." His voice wasn't quite steady. "And it makes me mad as hell. Why was that, Sabrina? Why? Why didn't he let us get close to him?"

She pressed her lips together against a sob and picked at a flaw in the fabric of the couch. At last she said slowly, "Because he was just too busy. He was too busy proving he could be as successful and make as much money as anyone in Mother's family had done. He was trying to forget he'd ever been poor and trying to make sure that we never would be. That took all of him, Martin. That's what caused the 'sudden' heart attack that killed him. That stress had been building for years and years."

He nodded. His eyes were dark with pain. "You're right. But it's hard to believe that he'll never have a chance to change his priorities."

"I know."

They traded tremulous smiles, comforted by sharing their sadness. Martin had always been her protective big brother, but being able to talk together about feelings, as equals, was a new experience. It was a nice one, she thought. Maybe she wasn't quite so alone after all.

For a few minutes they talked about childhood memories and the infrequent close times that they had shared with their parents. Then he said, "Where *is* Mom, anyway? I came by to ask if you and she might like to go out to dinner later."

"She's resting. I'm sure she'd love to go, but I can't. We'll do it another night."

"But there may not be another night. I'll be tied up with business meetings all the rest of this week and you'll be going back to San Francisco soon."

"No," she heard herself saying suddenly. "I don't think so. I'm seriously considering staying in Tulsa." The words seemed to reverberate off the walls. She sat very still, listening to them while she watched a reaction of pure surprise come into his face and felt the mirroring emotion build inside herself. She'd had no idea she was so close to making a decision about the major changes she'd been craving in her life, until she heard herself say the words. And just as suddenly as she'd said them, she knew that they were true. One of her decisions was made. She was going to stay in Tulsa.

"But, Sabrina! What about your career? What about your promotion to vice-president? You've been working for that recognition for six years!"

Sabrina stood and paced nervously over to the windowed wall. She stared out into the deep green of the trees.

"Six years that I should have spent working for something else."

"Like what?" He got up and came to her, worry etched in the fine lines around his eyes.

"Like finding myself...and finding someone to love."

She held out her hands to him then, feeling entirely defenseless, rawly vulnerable from the events of the past few days. His eyes searched her face; their unaccustomed closeness was still there.

"I'm restless, Martin," she blurted miserably. "I'm restless and lonely and I have to do *something*. I've known that for quite a while."

"But isn't it a little drastic to destroy your career and to give up your friends and the whole life you've made? Sabrina, we all feel that way sometimes, but you've worked so hard."

"This is different," she interrupted. "This goes deeper. The best thing for me to do is to come home again and get my bearings."

"You can't know that right now. You can't make any major decisions at all when basically you're still in shock over Dad's death. Give this some time, Sabrina, and it'll all work out."

"Only if I *do* something! Martin, I've felt this way before—during high school and right after college. I need a challenge, I need something new, something more out of life than I'm getting."

He was still frowning, but he chuckled softly and reached out to pinch her cheek as he used to do when she was a little girl and he was the idolized teenage brother.

"You sound like you're eighteen instead of twenty-eight," he teased, but his eyes told her that he understood. "If you'd come to dinner with me I'd give you a whole evening's worth of advice: all the wisdom I've been accumulating for thirty-seven years."

She smiled in spite of the frustrations pounding at her. "Let's have lunch tomorrow instead, okay? I'm going to the Cherokee drama at Tsa-La-Gi tonight and I need to go bathe and dress."

"Cherokee drama! With whom, if I may ask?"

"With Jarod Redfeather, a Cherokee. Don't you think that's appropriate?"

His attitude changed in a flash from indulgent to protective. "Who the hell is Jarod Redfeather? Where'd you meet him?"

"At the powwow last night. He—"

"He's a stranger!" he interrupted angrily. "You don't even know this guy and you're going off down into the hills with him, all the way to Tahlequah to a play that'll last half the night! Sabrina, if you want a date, call up some of your old friends; lots of them are still in Tulsa.''

She laughed and reached out to touch his arm. "You're sweet to be so concerned, Martin, and I love you for it, but I'll be perfectly all right. Remember that I'm all grown up now and I can take care of myself.''

"No, you can't. You proved that when you accepted a date with this character...whoever he is.''

"I'm just trying to learn a little bit about my own heritage...and yours,'' she said lightly, wishing he would smile. "I have to run and get ready now, but I promise to tell you all about the play at lunch tomorrow.''

He didn't reply.

She waited. "We do have a date for lunch, don't we?''

Finally he growled, "Yes.''

"What time are you coming by?''

"Eleven o'clock. You can't sleep half the day. You'd better get home early and go straight to bed.''

"Yes, sir!'' She saluted smartly. "I'll see you in the morning.''

At the doorway she stopped and turned to look at him. "Martin, don't worry. This'll just be an ordinary evening. There's absolutely nothing to worry about.''

But all the time she was trying to relax in her bath she wondered whether those words were true. She'd never admit it to Martin, but she was almost as apprehensive as he was about these plans she'd made with a stranger. It would probably be an interminable evening with a man she might not even be able to talk to. Last night, the light teasing she and Jarod had done was probably all they would ever have to say to each other.

Finally, she stepped out of the tub and took a bath sheet from the warming rack. She wrapped herself in it and slid open the door that led out to the deck, loving the intensity of the sun's heat after the cold air-conditioning of the house.

Well, she'd get through the evening as best she could, she thought resignedly as she brushed out her hair to dry. And no matter how awful it might be, tomorrow at lunch she'd tell Martin that it had been not only perfectly safe, but fascinating as well.

She tried to hold those realistic thoughts while she dressed, but underneath them was a beat, a rhythm, a purely emotional urgency made up of nothing but fantasy. By the time she heard the bell and left her room to go meet Jarod, all she could think about was seeing him again.

He waited for her, looking around the sumptuous foyer: at the gleaming tables with their arrangements of fresh flowers, at the old paintings in their heavy frames, at the ornate grandfather clock beside the door. He couldn't believe it, he thought for the thousandth time since he'd turned into the long, oak-lined drive. How could he have been so stupid as to be drawn to another woman from this world, another one of the silver-spooners that he scorned?

He tapped the toe of his boot impatiently against the marble floor. He wanted to hurry up and get this evening over with, to do what he'd promised he'd do and then bring Sabrina back here. After that, he'd never see her again. There was no way he'd be made a fool of twice in his life.

"Jarod, hello."

He turned. She was coming down the curving staircase, her black hair swinging past her face in a shining curtain. She was wearing something full and soft, all white and summery, and he felt his pulse quicken. He tightened his jaw. This was a one-time thing and he wasn't going to forget it.

"Sabrina." He was very solemn and there was a tension in his stance that hadn't been there the night before.

"Have I kept you waiting? I'm sorry. I heard the bell, but I had to look for my wrap." Her voice sounded breathlessly vapid in her own ears.

"No. I just got here." He still hadn't smiled at her.

Wonderful, she thought dryly. Just super. Last night had been some sort of fluke. This evening was going to be as horrible as she'd imagined.

Jackson, the houseman, materialized behind Jarod and showed them out onto the columned porch. They crossed to the top of the broad steps, then Jarod stopped.

"I had no idea," he said simply. He made a sweeping gesture that took in Jackson and the huge house behind them as well as the winding drive and rolling acres of wooded lawn in front of them.

"What do you mean?"

He shrugged and put his hand at the small of her back to guide her down the steps toward the gleaming new pickup truck. "I mean that this is just a little different from most of the places down in the hills where I come from."

"This house?"

"This everything." His tone lightened to one of wry humor. "Entirely different from things down on that reservation you were asking me about."

They reached the truck and he held the door for her, looking directly into her eyes. The glance held and at last he smiled at her.

He circled the vehicle and got in. "You know," he remarked thoughtfully as he started the motor, "I should've recognized the name Dante. My brother-in-law used to work for Dante Oil."

"Oh?" He seemed to be talking more to himself than to her.

"Yes. And I heard about your father. I'm sorry."

"Thank you."

The quiet words hung between them as he drove quickly down the long driveway. She wished that she could think of some other ones, words that could reach across the new, subtle distance that was separating them.

She folded her wrap and put it under her bag, then looked around her, searching for a way to break the silence. She examined the luxurious interior of the vehicle. "I like your truck," she said at last, as they left the old neighborhood for the expressway.

"Thanks. I had it customized so it'd be really comfortable for the times I take it on the road. But in a way it was a waste. Most of the time I fly."

"In your work? What do you do?"

"I rodeo. I'm a cowboy."

She grinned. "Isn't that something of a contradiction?"

He flashed a glance at her. "Being both a cowboy and an Indian?"

His crooked grin lit his face and her stomach fluttered. Maybe last night hadn't been a fluke after all.

He pretended to consider the question, then nodded. "It's not easy, but I can handle it."

"I'm sure there isn't much you *can't* handle," she murmured.

"So they tell me." He gave her a long, meaningful look before he turned his attention to gearing down for a slow car ahead.

The intense quality in his voice and the sexy glint in his eyes stirred her and began to recreate the spell he'd woven around her the night before with his smile and dancing. That same sensual awareness was vibrating in the air between them now; she saw it when he looked at her.

But there was something else in his eyes, too. He was sizing her up in a way she didn't understand.

"And what do you do?" he was asking. "Your card said Harwell and Neel's, but not what you do for them."

"Almost anything. I've worked for the chain for six years and I've been everything from furniture and art buyer to division director for both men's and women's clothing. I've worked mostly in clothing; that's my favorite.''

He looked at her, genuinely interested in every word. "And that's what you're doing now?"

"Yes," she answered quickly. Then she remembered. "Well, no."

He laughed. "And you call *me* a contradiction."

She laughed, too. "That's what I was doing when I left San Francisco three weeks ago, but I've decided not to go back."

His dark eyes flashed away from the road and back to her again. "What are you going to do?"

"Oh . . . I think I may buy a little boutique or start some kind of shop of my own. That's been a vague dream in the back of my mind for a long time. I'd love to see if I could make it work—I think it'd be heavenly to have complete control of everything from stock to finances."

He chuckled wryly. "Heavenly isn't exactly the word I'd choose. This past couple of weeks the whole merchandising racket's been more like hell for me."

"What do you mean? What do you have to do with merchandising?"

"I'm trying to start a store. Western wear and saddles and other tack."

"In Tulsa?"

"Right. Over on Memorial. The building's nearly done and some of the stock's already been shipped. It's scheduled to open in a month or so."

"But how're you going to manage that and be gone to rodeos all the time, too?"

"That's exactly what I've been asking myself." His laugh was ironic. "Ever since the manager I'd hired quit last week."

"Oh. You had a manager. You weren't planning to quit rodeo?"

"Not now. I'd planned to rodeo the rest of this season at least. Thirty-four's too old for getting bucked off and kicked around all the time, but I might even stay with it one more season after this one."

"And then you'll run the store?"

"I hope not!" His voice was horrified. "I'd hate it and it'd probably go under besides. It's just an investment for me, one that I don't know a whole lot about. When I leave the circuit I'm going to breed racehorses."

"Do you have a ranch?"

He nodded. "Down here not too far from the 'reservation,'" he said with a teasing glance at her. "I'll show it to you sometime."

He forced his eyes away from her cameo profile and stared straight ahead. Now *why* had he said that? He wasn't going to ask her out again.

But the sound of her voice drove the thought from his mind, and for the rest of the trip they talked easily about his store and her job.

Sabrina relaxed, drinking in the sight of the rolling green hills that cradled the narrow winding route of Highway 51 and the blue expanse of the Grand Lake O' the Cherokees when they crossed it. By the time they arrived at the large Cherokee cultural complex site called Tsa-La-Gi she had completely forgotten that there was a possibility the evening could be anything but wonderful.

They wandered through the thickly growing trees and around the scattered buildings and old ruins until dusk, unconsciously keeping to themselves. They talked about the Cherokee history books she'd bought and about his own family's customs; she told him a little bit about her family and her discovery that her father had been on the Cherokee rolls.

Finally he suggested that they have a quick supper at the hot dog stand near the gate to the ancient village.

"Let's go in," she suggested as they took the food from the vendor.

"It's too late now. We'll come back again sometime soon," Jarod heard himself saying, to his own complete consternation. "It'll take a whole day to do justice to the village and the museum."

He couldn't think of a great deal to say as they finished the simple meal, and when they began to follow the growing crowd of playgoers down the winding gravelled path toward the amphitheater he walked a little apart from her. He'd been thrown off onto his head by one too many broncs, he thought. He was losing it completely. One minute he was vowing never to see this woman again and the next he was promising to bring her back here, to take her to his ranch, to spend a day with her.

Memories flashed through his mind as they entered the theater and began to descend its steep steps. That long-ago experience with Diane Medford had taught him to stay away from rich girls for whom he was only a curiosity. He'd better remember that lesson.

The drama began with a burst of cannon fire and a line of actor-soldiers running full speed down the face of the steep bluff that formed the backdrop for the stage. Their footing was invisible and Sabrina gasped, reaching reflexively for Jarod's hand as if her holding on to him could keep the young men from falling to the hard ground below.

He was strangely still. She glanced up at him, starting to withdraw her hand in the same movement.

But he wouldn't let her. His touch became warm and enveloping in that instant and his eyes burned into hers through the darkness.

From that moment she had trouble keeping her mind on the play; when he laced her fingers through his in a gesture as sensual as the full moon rising behind the half-naked medicine man at the top of the rocky ridge, she gave it up completely. The conflict on stage was Cherokee against white and Cherokee against Cherokee, but she couldn't think in terms of anything that broad. She could think only of one man and one woman and the warmth of hands intertwined for an hour that had the power to drive away years of lonely cold.

They didn't talk at all as they climbed the high stairs to the exit, and, their hands still firmly clasped, they separated themselves from the rest of the audience as soon as they could. They left the lighted path and started back through the woods toward the truck, silently choosing their way by an instinct as old as the one that was keeping her hand still cradled in his.

The night was deepening and the oppressive heat had begun to lift at last. She felt a light breeze stir her hair and Jarod reached out to touch it.

They stopped to look at each other in the faint moonlight sifting through a narrow opening in the trees. She walked into his arms; his lips took hers the second she got there, capturing them with a sweetness as intense as the soaring, rushing joy that had sprung to life in some unknown primitive part of her.

She gave her mouth to him with an instinctive wanting that was completely new; she parted her lips to his and met his questing tongue with hers. She returned its sweetly savage insistence from a well of passion hidden deep within her, with a tempestuousness that had never before been touched. She caught it, finally, in the honeyed trap of her lips to hold and torment it with tiny teasings, and she trembled while she drank in the taste of him.

He pulled her closer. He held her against him with open, honest wanting, letting the desire that had been born in him the minute he saw her face feed on the tantalizing fragrance of her hair and the soft pliancy of her slender body. He wanted to sink into those sensations and into the mystery of her.

He took back his tongue and then thrust it deeper into her mouth as if he were demanding to know all her secrets. His sinewy power rocketed through her and its ravening depth grew stronger by the second. Her chest constricted almost beyond endurance and she inhaled a breath heavy with his musky, masculine smell and with the pungent scents of the sultry summer night.

At last, slowly, reluctantly, the kiss was over, and they stood a little distance apart. She looked up into his eyes, at his handsome mouth that had the power to burn its shape into her very soul.

He was looking at her in the shadowy light, smiling a bit sadly, shaking his head in wonder and affirmation like a wise, bronzed god acknowledging a whole new reality here on the old sacred ground.

Then he brought her back to him for another kiss and another and another until he had set her blood on fire.

Chapter Three

They couldn't keep from touching, even though they were separated by the bucket seats of the pickup; in the aftermath of their fervent kisses an almost unbearable tension was pulsing between them like a live wire. Jarod drove with his eyes on the dark, twisting line of the highway, but hers kept coming back to the moon-shadowed profile of his face, her mind completely filled by the memory of his mouth on hers.

Coming around a curve in the road, he slowed and she looked ahead to see a graveled lane branching away from the pavement. "My cabin's just about a mile over that way. Want to drop by there for a night-cap and a tour of my breechclout-and-feather collection?"

The smile in his voice made her look at him again; its curve on his lips made her ache to taste his kisses. She had a vague intimation that she should say no, a shred of thought floating out from the remnant of her mind still strong enough to function, but the wild feelings flowing through her obliterated it.

"You don't have a collection of etchings?"

"I don't," he admitted solemnly, the smile still in his voice. He twisted the wheel with his left hand, his right one tightened around hers as the thick tires crunched on gravel. "Breechclouts and feathers and a few turkey-feather fans will have to do."

They followed the dirt road a short distance, then stopped at a metal gate. He punched a button on his sun visor and it swung open; they went through to a dirt road leading across an expanse of moonlit meadow.

"Oh, Jarod, it's beautiful!" she breathed, her vision captured by the yellow glimmer of the magic night.

He nodded, tightening his hold on her hand. "God's country. I'd never live anyplace else."

At the far side of the huge grassy bowl the track started up through thick stands of trees. It led up and up, then around to a sudden clearing at its summit where a log cabin swept into view in the glow of the headlights. It sprawled, low and solid, nestled into the treed, rocky hillside behind it.

He stopped the truck under a canopy of branches and turned off the motor. Even before its sound died away in the silence they came together hungrily, desperately, as if neither of them could have waited another second, their mouths finding each other with unerring instinct. They kissed once, with deep haste, their tongues entwining, caressing, communicating need and pure desire, knowledge and awareness that words could not have reached.

Then he took his lips away from her mouth, removed his hands from her back and left her alone, bereft, while he got out of the truck and came around it to touch her again. She was out of the vehicle, walking beside him along a path she knew vaguely to be paved with stones. Her only surety was the warmth of his hand in the sensitive small of her back.

Dimly she was aware of the steep bluff dropping away from the front of the house. In the moonlight the view was spectacular; shimmering moonbeams danced on the water of a lake below. Summer night sounds, locusts and birds, floated to them on the breeze along with scents of grass and pines and horses; she heard them, but the sound of which she was most conscious was that of Jarod's breathing and the click of his boot heels on the stones as they walked.

Suddenly she felt as if she were two people. One part of her was more open to simply being than she'd ever thought possible, the other was unable to absorb even the sensations of sight, sound or scent for the overwhelming ones of taste and feel: the taste of his kiss still on her lips and the feel of his hard, callused hand through the thin fabric of her blouse.

At the first step of the porch he stopped and turned to her, putting his hand under her chin to tilt her face up to his. "Sabrina..."

The sound was more a breath than a word and it trembled in her ear, on her skin. She raised her arms to put them around his neck, but they stopped on the broad curve of his massive shoulders, her hands fascinated by the solid column of his neck. Her fingers stroked the silky hair that touched his collar, then moved slowly, slowly, around to shape his ear and trace tiny circles behind and below it.

His eyes were on hers, and here where there were no trees to obstruct the moon's brightness she could see their expression clearly. They were intensely dark with the desire and wonder that had been in the sound of her name on his lips. But they held a question, too.

Instinctively she moved toward him, her arms intending to draw him back into the enchantment and wipe away the query.

He held her away from him, though, his hands loosely powerful at each side of her waist.

She moved infinitesimally closer to him and the tips of her breasts brushed the hard muscles of his chest.

He bent his head to kiss her.

He kissed her lightly, almost hesitantly, standing there in the pool of yellow light, then he started up the steps, holding her beside him in the circle of his arm. They crossed the porch and he let her into the house without turning on a light. She had impressions of rustic space and wood and glass, and then of the deep, smooth cushions of a couch, but his closeness was still the dominant force in her consciousness and she couldn't really see anything but him.

He turned to her and the room became a high-ceilinged haven created just for them. Behind them was a wall of window to let the moonlight pour in. They touched hands, then cheeks, then he was stroking the bare skin of her arms while she traced the corded muscles across the back of his shoulders.

They touched with swift, soft, exploratory caresses, her hands on his face, the high fine cheekbones and aquiline nose; his on the narrowness of her waist, the wings of her shoulder blades, the tantalizing shape of her slim hips under the thin skirt.

Then his full lips were hot against her cheek and she was melting, lying back into the depth of the leather cushions. His mouth came back to hers to take it and brand it with his lips.

She dissolved into him with an abandon born of the new profligate feelings that he created in her; she gave her tongue to his stroking as if she were freezing and could not live without the fire it held. He explored the recesses of her mouth with an urgent thoroughness, pressing her body ever closer to the length of his.

She impelled him to meld them even tighter with importunate caresses of his tongue with hers, fierce throbbing touches that begged him to learn that and everything else about her.

At last they broke apart. She was bruised by the force of the kiss, breathless with the hammering rhythms of their hearts beating together. One of his hands was at her back, holding her to him as if he were afraid she might move away, and the other was roaming over her shoulders and up onto the skin at the nape of her neck, an insistently tantalizing sensation.

Then it began to move with a more definite purpose, becoming an unparalleled tempter spreading hot flame down the length of her backbone and around the soft curve of her hips, coming back to wrap her rib cage in its heat. It found the trembling softness of her breast and enclosed it in a cloud of fire, its fingers coming to the swollen thrusting tip as if it were coming home.

The galvanizing rapture spiraled through to her loins as he teased and caressed her, impelling her to ask for more.

She breathed one word, "Jarod..." then reached to pull him on top of her. The warm intimacy of his weight, and the aching shaft of wanting that it sharpened in her, plunged straight to her very core.

She moaned and floated deeper into the softness of the leather, a peculiar satisfaction rushing through her underneath the intense sensuality, a mindless fulfillment as if she had found not only the delicious thrill of danger, but a shelter, too, at last. This man, this place, this incredible delight was what she had been looking for all of her life.

The idea shocked her back to reality.

She twisted under him and tried to free her mouth from his, but he wouldn't let her go. He finished the kiss, trailing the gossamer touch of the tip of his tongue along the outline of her lips. Even in the midst of resisting him she turned her face to follow it.

"Sabrina? What is it?" His breath feathered against her cheek.

She struggled to sit up. "Jarod. I . . . I can't. This is too soon." She moved a little away from the hollow his weight was making in the cushions, trying to distance herself from the closeness that still seemed the most natural comfort in the world. "It's just that we hardly know each other, and . . ."

And you terrify me. The words pounded in her pulse beat. You're an exhilaration and a refuge and everything I've ever needed and if I made love with you I could never let you out of my sight again.

He was silent, completely still.

She thought of the wall that had been between them at the beginning of the evening. Now she was the one who was putting it there, but she couldn't help it. The feelings he aroused in her were too dangerous, she was too vulnerable to handle this right now.

She couldn't look at him; she stared at the saffron moon just outside the wall of windows. She felt him get up.

"I'm sorry," he said. He crossed the room to switch on a light.

When Jarod spoke again it was with dry self-mockery.

"I must've been succumbing to the savagery that some Indians are said to be prone to."

His face, thrown into relief by the soft glow of the lamp, was smoothly expressionless. "I guess I just forgot that you're only one-sixteenth."

Now the mockery included her, too.

Sabrina looked back at him, unable to smile, and her lips trembled. She felt the sting of tears behind her eyes. She had pulled away from him with the last shred of strength left in her, and now she couldn't bear the loss of his warmth.

Shakily, she stood. She had to get out of here, away from him, had to end this shattering evening that now had come full circle.

"I have to go now," she said, her voice hardly more than a whisper. "I really need to be getting home."

At first he didn't answer. He was simply watching, his eyes darker and less readable than ever.

"You're tired," he said at last. He glanced at his watch. "It's almost two. Why don't we wait until morning to drive back?"

"But, Jarod..."

"You'll take the bed," he interrupted, indicating the open door of the bedroom, "and I'll sleep here on the couch." His tone was as dispassionate as if he were a bellboy showing her to a hotel room.

She hesitated. He was right. She *was* totally exhausted. At this moment the long drive sounded like torture; it would mean another two hours alone with him while he played havoc with her emotions.

"My mother will be expecting me."

"Call her." He gestured toward the phone.

Reflexively, she looked at her own watch. "It's so late, I'm sure she's asleep, and so are the servants. I'd just disturb the entire household."

He nodded. "I promise to have you there in the morning before they even know you haven't come in."

She let him show her into the bedroom and closed the door. She listened to him moving about the living room while she slipped out of her clothing. Her limbs felt like lead.

The long days and nights just past had drained her. They'd been so filled with shock and sadness, with worry about her mother, with the momentous decisions she herself was making and with the excitement, sexuality and strange sense of coming home that Jarod had created in her.

She forced the thoughts from her mind as she stretched out on the bed. She closed her ears and eyes and willed the blackness of sleep to take her.

Sabrina awoke to an early-morning breeze that already carried the heat of summer. She pushed the sheet away and stirred, drowsily unsure of her whereabouts in those hazy seconds between sleeping and waking.

The log wall facing her filled her vision, its hard horizontal lines softened by circular turkey-feather fans and a woven hanging. A lethal-looking bow hung on the other side of the wide door. A coil of rope was on the floor.

Jarod. She was in Jarod's house, in his bed.

Memories of the evening before came flooding back; memories of his arms, his lips, of the strange sense of homecoming she'd felt.

She sat up and reached for her clothes, uncomfortable even with remembering the range and depth of her emotions. How could she have come even that close to making love with a perfect stranger?

Everything in this room was completely alien to her. How could she have felt so close to him, imagined that she belonged with him?

Rapidly, she began to dress. Last night had happened only because she'd been so in need of comfort and closeness, and now that she knew that, she wouldn't let it happen again. He had too much power over her, the power to touch her very soul.

They were too different to ever have a relationship, her thought continued, racing in rhythm with her fingers as she closed the rows of tiny buttons on her blouse. He had hinted at that when he picked her up yesterday and he'd been right.

She would ask Jarod to drive her back to Tulsa immediately and that would be that; she wouldn't see him again. If all the problems she'd been having lately had caused this much damage to her judgment, then she'd better not see him or anyone else until she'd recovered.

But she opened her door to the sight of his rumpled linens on the couch and his boots dropped on the floor beside it. Her eyes went to the hollow his body had left in the deep cushions. The desire to feel the long strength of it against hers again hit her like a blow.

"Sabrina?"

She turned. He was silhouetted against the morning light in the doorway to the kitchen, the breadth of his shoulders filling it. "Good morning, Jarod."

"Good morning. I thought you might be up by the time I finished feeding the horses." He crossed the room toward her and she felt her breathing quicken. He didn't come near her, however; he bent to pick up the boots and sat down in a chair to change into them from the battered ones he was wearing.

"Who feeds them when you aren't here?" She was pleased not only that her voice was steady, but that her brain seemed to be functioning once more.

"My nephew." He flashed her a quick glance, "Angie's brother."

He tugged out of one boot, then got up and limped into the bedroom. "How about breakfast before we start the long trek back?" he called over his shoulder.

"Are you cooking?"

He chuckled and she felt the warm rush of camaraderie that they'd shared before.

"No," he said, coming back with a bootjack. "There's a café right after we get on Highway 51. It's sort of a cross between a burger joint and a truck stop, but the biscuits are great."

"All right. But before we go I need to call home."

"Help yourself."

She crossed to the phone and dialed, then her eyes went back to Jarod. She couldn't help watching the fluid grace of his movements, the sinewy pull of his thigh muscles under the thin denim of his jeans as he fit his heel into the wooden jack and shrugged out of the other boot. His jeans were faded almost white but they were immaculate, and his shirt was of a crisp blue-and-white checked fabric that contrasted with his skin and made him look more than ever like a bronzed god.

He was wearing that same self-assured air this morning, too, the aura that she'd noticed when they met. He was all together and filled with purpose; he obviously knew what *he* wanted to accomplish that day.

He finished with the boots and sat watching her, waiting.

She wasn't going to get away with it, he thought. She could be as crisp and noncommittal as she wanted this morning, but she wasn't going to kiss him the way she had last night and then just get up and walk right out of his life.

He'd lain awake for hours thinking about it. About her. The taste of her wouldn't leave his tongue; her scent had clung to him and to the pillows of the couch. He'd relived the curving heat of her body in his arms, her laughter at the powwow, her intensity at the drama.

The cold feeling of loss he'd felt when she'd pulled away from him had flowed through him again, too, and around four in the morning he'd made a decision. He'd been wrong about the lesson he'd learned from Diane Medford. He wasn't going to stay away from Sabrina. He was just going to make sure that this time *he* was the one in control.

Jackson finally answered and she gave him a message for her mother; she was fine and would be home before noon. She hung up.

"Everything all right?"

"Fine. I don't think Mother has even missed me, so there's no problem."

They walked out to the truck together, but apart, the tumultuous emotions that had held them close on this same path the night before lost somehow in the harsh sunlight. He headed the pickup down the winding road. She glanced back at the cabin.

"Jarod, it's a beautiful place," she said. "All tucked behind the trees like this, it's like a secret hideaway, one that's been here for years and years."

He nodded.

"It's only been here for five years or so, but it *is* my secret hideout. It's the place that keeps me sane."

Fleetingly she wondered whom else he had brought there; was a different girl available to share this refuge with him each time he came home from the rodeo circuit?

Mentally she shrugged. Even if there were, it made no difference to her. She was going to breakfast with him and that was all. Once they got back to Tulsa she'd never see him again.

Deliberately she turned her thoughts to her own affairs as they crossed the sun-washed meadow and closed the gate behind them. She'd call San Francisco later today and take a leave of absence, she decided. And then she'd start looking around for the best location for her shop. She'd keep very, very busy, she'd call some of her old friends and soon she'd recover her equilibrium.

He turned to glance at her after he'd pulled the truck out onto the highway. "Well, what's on your agenda for the day? How far along are the plans for your shop?''

She hesitated, startled that he seemed to be reading her mind. ''Oh, I...I'm just beginning to think about it. I don't even know what location I want yet.'' She opened her bag to look for her sunglasses. ''You said your store is over on Memorial?''

''Yes. Just south of Forty-first. You may have seen it—white adobe, one side slanting lower than the other, brown beams and pillars—the outside's finished.''

She shook her head. ''I haven't been over that way.''

''I just hope we can get the inside done and the stock and staff all squared away so it'll open on time.''

''I'm sure it will. Once you find another manager all that'll fall into place pretty fast.''

He glanced at her, then looked back at the road. ''Sabrina, how about *you*? Would you come in to be my manager?''

She stared at him, astonished. Trying to absorb both the idea and the abruptness of his words, she let them tremble in the air between them, transparent in the slant of morning sunlight that filled the cab. He was looking straight ahead, his hands relaxed on the wheel, but she could feel the quiet, coiled waiting inside him.

He knew it, too, she thought. Her answer to that question would determine much more than the next move in her career and the fate of his store. It would decide whether they would ever see each other again.

She tried to talk herself out of accepting. ''But Jarod, I...I don't know a thing about Western wear.

And it's really too soon for me to make a definite career move. My decision to come back to Tulsa is new—only a couple of days old. I need some time before I do *anything*."

She listened to herself, appalled. Why wasn't she refusing? This waffling was insane. She had to say no, definitely no, and mean it. She couldn't have a professional relationship with him without wanting a personal one, too.

"I guess Western wear isn't too different from any other kind of clothing business," he said, slowing the vehicle to enter the parking lot of a small café. "You'd have to learn about tack, but I could help you with that and I know some other people who could, too." He stopped the truck and cut the motor. It was very quiet.

Finally she said, "It'd be a lot to handle all at once. Probably too much."

"Not for you." He sounded very certain, as if he'd just made the decision for her.

He opened his door and got out, coming around to escort her into the bustling café.

What was she doing? she thought helplessly as she slid into a booth beneath the windows. Of *course* she couldn't work for him!

"Jarod, I couldn't possibly..."

"You couldn't possibly refuse," he interrupted, turning on the full force of his boyish charm, complete with beguiling charm.

The waitress came to take their orders and as soon as she'd gone, he began his argument in earnest.

"Look, Sabrina, this is the perfect situation. You've just decided to stay in Tulsa and you don't have a job. I have to have a manager, very soon, and I have no idea where to get one."

He smiled at her, the crooked grin that melted her insides. "If you say no, I don't know what I'll do. I'll lose thousands of dollars because the store won't open on time, I'll hire worthless, lazy employees who'll steal me blind, I'll buy all the wrong stock and customers will never come back a second time, I'll..."

She began to laugh. "You'll get along just fine," she contradicted. "You'll go to an employment agency who'll find you a good manager and you won't have to worry about another thing."

He shook his head and poured her coffee from the pot near his elbow. "I doubt that." He poured his own coffee and fixed her with a solemn look as he sipped at it. "Sabrina, look at it this way. If you don't like it you don't have to stay forever. This can be a temporary thing for you if you want it to be; you can work for me for six months, a year, and then open up your own shop. You don't have to give up your dreams for this."

But "this" may generate a whole new set of dreams, she thought. Dreams that will be infinitely harder to give up.

"Just think," he went on. "You can learn on *my* store—make all your mistakes on it—and then *yours* will run that much more smoothly from the very start."

She smiled and shook her head in amused dismay. She had to tell him no. An unequivocal no. How could she even consider working with him, being with him all the time? If they were together, if he kissed her again, touched her again the way he had last night, she knew they would end up making love. She'd never be strong enough to resist a second time. And if they did make love...if she spent a night in his arms...she would do something totally insane like falling in love with him.

Their food came, heaping plates of eggs and potatoes, bacon, biscuits and gravy, and she seized it as a distraction. "Good heavens, Jarod, I can never eat all this!"

"You'd better. You're going to need your strength. That store has about a year's worth of work that has to be done in the next few weeks."

She laughed. "You are *impossible*! I haven't said I'm going to manage your store."

"Oh." He flashed the teasing grin again. "I thought silence gave consent. Well, then," he said, as he began to attack the food, "I'll give you until we get to Tulsa to decide. Think it over carefully until we drive up to your front door. Then you can tell me yes or no. I'm leaving tomorrow to go back on the circuit and I have to have a manager before I go."

She burst into laughter. "I cannot *believe* this! You're conducting business in the most haphazard way I've ever seen. Jarod, this is a big investment you're making! You can't just go around hiring managers off the street from among people you've only known for a couple of days...."

His sensual lips curved in a smile that turned his eyes to amber. "That's exactly why I need you so badly," he drawled innocently. "Don't you see? I'm a cowboy and a horseman, not a businessman. I don't have the foggiest idea of what I'm doing with a store."

Was there another meaning in the words "I need you so badly" or did she hear it there because they set free an echo in her pounding blood? She tore her eyes away from his and fastened them on a burly trucker who was feeding coins into the jukebox. She took a bite of her food, swallowed it without tasting and tried to fit the words "No, Jarod, I can't accept your offer" around her tongue.

The bluegrass song that the trucker had chosen came spilling loudly into the room and she listened to it. As soon as it was over she'd give Jarod her answer. She'd be very logical, very firm. She didn't need to wait until they got to Tulsa.

His rough hand closed over hers. "What are you thinking?" he asked. "Are you going to accept?"

She lifted her eyes to his, the refusal on the tip of her tongue.

But the lonely minor notes of the song shimmered on the shaft of sunlight that came spilling through the window to fall across their table and his smile destroyed her.

Wordlessly she nodded.

Chapter Four

Sabrina opened her door as soon as Jarod stopped the pickup in the wide circle drive. "Don't bother to see me in. I'll be fine."

"All right." He shifted into park and left the motor idling, leaning casually on the wheel. "Shall we meet at the store? About nine-thirty tomorrow morning?"

His tone wasn't quite as relaxed as he looked; she could hear a note of tension that matched the tautness in hers. Was he sensing the doubts she felt, or was he having some late misgivings of his own?

They'd spent the drive back to Tulsa making detailed plans for the store and for the contract defining their business relationship; all that had made Jarod's sudden job offer and her impulsive "yes" begin to seem very serious. So had the obvious but unmentioned fact that they would be working and spending time together. There was no way to make detailed plans for that.

Well, it was too late to get out of it now, she thought. She'd given her word. But the terms of the contract were for only six months; after that, if things weren't working out, she'd be free.

Or would she?

She pushed the thought away. "Nine-thirty will be fine. See you then."

She stepped out, smiling her goodbye. She closed the door behind and ran up the steps without looking back.

The tall oak panels swung apart before she touched them; Jackson was waiting for her.

"Good morning, Jackson. Has my mother come down yet?"

"Not yet, Miss Sabrina. But your brother is waiting for you on the terrace."

Puzzled, she glanced at her watch. "He's early. We were going to lunch, but not until eleven-thirty."

Martin was pacing back and forth at the edge of the flagstone terrace, a coffee cup in his hand. A table with a white cloth was set on the east side of the terrace under the sweeping willow trees; her mother loved to breakfast outside in summer.

Her brother swung to face her. "Sabrina!"

"Hi, Martin. Aren't you early?"

"The question is, aren't you late?"

The irritation in his tone surprised her. She looked at him more closely; he was clearly angry.

"No . . . I called," she replied defensively. "I talked to Jackson early this morning and left a message for Mother."

"Well, you might have tried doing that last night. You could have saved us all a night's sleep."

"Martin, what *are* you talking about? Would you please stop talking in riddles?" She dropped her bag and wrap on a wrought-iron bench and crossed to the table, trying to shift her thoughts away from the business of the store and from Jarod.

"I'm talking about Mother's being awake all night worrying about you. She's hardly been able to sleep since Dad died, and your staying out all night certainly didn't help."

Sharp guilt stabbed through her. "I'm sorry! Martin, you know I wouldn't have worried her for anything." She poured herself some icy orange juice from a carafe and sat down, motioning him to sit, too. He came closer but remained standing across from her.

She searched his face. "We didn't decide to stay the night until nearly two o'clock and I knew everyone would be asleep by then."

"Mother wasn't. She called me at 3:00 A.M., worried sick that you'd been in an accident or something."

"Oh, Martin, I'm so sorry," she repeated helplessly. Her throat was dry; she took a sip of the cold juice. "I wish I'd called. I thought all the time we'd be back here by two at the latest, but . . ."

He dropped into the chair opposite her and distractedly ran his hand through his immaculately groomed hair. "Look, Sabrina," he said, his voice harsh. "What're you doing running around all over the state and staying out all night with some man you don't even know?"

"He's a cowboy," she retorted airily, trying to lighten the atmosphere.

"That just makes it worse."

The censure in his voice grated on her tired nerves. "Oh, come on, Martin, give me a break! What kind of provincialism *is* this?"

He continued as if he hadn't heard her. "And he's somebody you'll *never* know, Sabrina." He leaned across the table toward her. "Provincial attitude or not, I know what I'm talking about." Every word was weighted for emphasis. "There's no way you have one single thing in common with this guy, and you never will. I can't believe you went out with him, much less spent the night."

She glared at him, furious now. He was intruding on her life just as he'd done when she was sixteen! How did he think she'd survived all the years since then without his direction?

"I'm perfectly capable of making decisions about where I spend the night!" she replied hotly.

He shrugged and slumped deeper into his chair. "That seems to be a matter of opinion."

Fatigue and sadness were stronger than the anger in his voice, and her own irritation began to drain away. The streak of silver hair at his temple glinted in the sunlight; she'd never noticed before how much he looked like their father.

"Martin, you're sterotyping," she said more softly. "You ought to meet Jarod. You'd like him."

"No, thanks. We couldn't talk to each other, there'd be absolutely nothing to say."

He tugged absently at the lock of hair that had fallen onto his forehead, then impatiently brushed it back. "Sabrina, I'm really concerned about you. First that sudden decision to quit your job and move back to Tulsa and now this Indian cowboy...."

She reached for his hand, needing that comforting new closeness that they'd shared the day before.

"Martin. Dear Martin. Please don't worry. I've been making all my own decisions for quite a few years now. Remember that."

"Well, right now you're making them awfully fast and without giving them a whole lot of thought," he said worriedly. "You need somebody to give you some perspective. I'm still your big brother, and don't you forget it!" He paused and his frown deepened. "And this Jarod character had better not forget it, either!"

She chuckled. "I promise that if my honor is impugned in any way, you'll be the first to know."

The teasing words made him smile, but his eyes were still worried. He squeezed her hand. "Truly, Sabrina, I didn't come over here this morning to give you a lecture. I know you're an adult now... I think."

They laughed together. "I know." She smiled her forgiveness. "You really came over to take me to lunch."

He looked stricken. "I'm sorry, little sister. We have to cancel lunch. That's the reason I came by. The representatives from that company in Houston are coming in early—they're arriving at the airport at noon and I have to meet them." He released her hand and walked around the table to stand beside her.

"But there's one good thing: they'll be leaving early, too. We can go to lunch tomorrow." He ruffled her hair. "Same time? Eleven-thirty?"

She pushed back her chair and stood up, trying to think of a fictitious reason to refuse. This was the world's worst time to tell him that she'd committed herself to working for Jarod. That news would ruin things all over again.

She put her arm through his and began walking him toward the house. "I can't have lunch tomorrow," she said casually, "But I'll call you in the evening and we'll set up another time."

He stopped and made her face him. "Why can't you go to lunch? Do you have another date with this Jarod?"

"'This Jarod,'" she quoted. "You keep calling him 'this Jarod.' His name isn't 'this.' It's simply Jarod Redfeather."

The distraction didn't work. He persisted. "*Do* you have a date with him?"

She sighed and gave up. "I'm going to work for him. I have to meet him at the store tomorrow morning and I'm sure we'll work right through lunch. There'll be only a few hours to get me informed about the essentials before he has to leave for the rodeo circuit again."

He stared at her, astounded. "What the hell are you talking about? What does a cowboy have to do with a store?"

"He's investing in a Western wear store," she explained. "I've agreed to manage it for him."

He said nothing, continuing to listen as if she'd spoken in a foreign language and he needed a translation.

She looked up at him, her eyes pleading with him to understand.

Finally he exploded. "Sabrina, has this guy got you mesmerized? You've known him for . . . what? . . . two days? Forty-eight hours? One powwow and one play, and you're staying out all night with him and accepting a job from him?"

"I know what I'm doing," she replied, turning away. She started to move toward the door again. "Martin, don't worry." She tapped the thin watch on his wrist. "It's getting late; you have to be at the airport."

He was still standing in the same spot, staring at her, his handsome face filled with frustration. She had to get him out of here so she could think.

"Martin, we can talk some more tomorrow night. I'll call you. I promise. Maybe we can go to the club."

She got him through the house and out the door at last. Then she walked back through the dim coolness of the hallway and into the bright sunlight on the terrace. She'd defended her decisions and all her recent actions, but inside she was just as bewildered by them as Martin was. Her life was changing so fast that the images in her mind looked like a kaleidoscope in the brilliance of the morning.

She picked up her things from the bench and went back into the house, hurrying now as if she could escape from her thoughts. Martin was right. It was as if Jarod had mesmerized her, as if he had magically unlocked the wild emotions that had been coursing just under the surface all her life. Now they were surging free and they were carrying her away.

When she reached the stairs she began to run. All she wanted now was the haven of her room.

Jarod awoke even earlier than usual and ran from Forty-first Street to Fifty-first and back again. It was a dangerous place to run and he was glad; he concentrated on finding a path and on the movements of the traffic, his mind firmly fixed on the present every second of the time.

When he returned to the store he did yoga and worked out on his weight machine. He kept at it until nine twenty-five when he stepped into the shower. He pushed away all awareness of the time and deliberately relaxed under the hot spray, focusing his thoughts on his physical conditioning and on the rides he had drawn for that night and the next day.

At last he stepped out and began to dress. He'd avoided this moment as long as he could. He would walk into the office and Sabrina would either be there or she wouldn't. She seemed to be a woman who would keep her word, but you never could tell. They hadn't yet signed anything and the position she'd have didn't compare to the company vice presidency that she'd mentioned.

If she'd changed her mind she'd probably have called, but the easiest thing to do would be simply not to show up, to leave him waiting. People did that sometimes to avoid painful explanations. Diane had taught him that a long time ago.

Sabrina moved briskly through the huge open space of the store, making notes on her clipboard while she tried to visualize the finished interior. She might as well be doing something while she waited for Jarod, she thought. After all, she arrived at the store this morning determined to concentrate on business.

She glimpsed her reflection in the hat department mirror; she certainly *looked* like business. She'd dressed in a suit, as was her custom for work, and had pulled her hair back into a chignon. It made her feel that this was definitely a professional meeting and not another date.

She took off the huge tortoiseshell glasses she used for reading and looked around her again. Workmen were swarming all over the place, building counters and installing racks and glass, painting the walls, finishing the floor. She could see no way they could open for three weeks, at least. It would probably take longer.

There'd be plenty to do to keep her mind off Jarod, she thought involuntarily. She could bury herself in the details of getting this store off the ground and forget what it had been like in his arms. She hoped.

I have to forget him as a man, at least for a while, she thought as she went over to inspect the tile that a workman was laying in the entryway. A new job and readjusting to an old city were enough for her right now. She had to hold her feelings for Jarod at bay.

She was talking with the workman when Jarod walked up behind her.

"Think there's any hope?"

She whirled to look at him, already warmed by the sound of his voice. Concentrate, Sabrina, she told herself, fighting the insidious intimacy. Keep it business.

"I'm not too sure," she said, her tone coming out a bit sharper than she'd intended. "I was just asking if this tile could be finished tomorrow, but evidently it can't."

Jarod didn't respond. He looked down at the man laying tile. "Morning, Sam. How's it going?"

The two men talked briefly, then Jarod began moving away, gesturing for Sabrina to come with him. "You're not wasting any time, are you?"

His manner seemed somehow accusatory and she bristled. "I've been making some notes while I waited."

"Well, keep it to notes and don't bug the workmen, okay?"

She stared at him. "I'm the manager and I'm not supposed to bug the workmen?"

"I'll take care of the construction," he said flatly. "You worry about the stock and the personnel."

The order made sense, but it created a quick anger in her. "Look, Jarod, all I did was..."

"I heard you," he interrupted, but his tone was placating now. "It's just that I know all these guys, Sabrina. I had the contractor hire them. I'll take care of them and you take care of the store. Okay?" He smiled into her eyes.

She put her glasses back on and stared down at the notepad, trying to find her control. The effort was made even more difficult by the fact that, in spite of her resentment, she had unconsciously moved a little closer to him. His hair was curling damply at the back of his neck, the smell of soap was on his skin; that and the crisp freshness of his shirt made her want to touch him.

She looked up at him.

"I might be able to take better care of the store if you'd show up on time. In case you haven't noticed, you're late."

The reproach annoyed him. A retort rose to his lips, but then he looked into her eyes and it died. Those glasses made her eyes huge and even more beautiful—blue-gray skies to be lost in. She was a different person somehow, with them on, and wearing that suit and with her hair fixed like that. Different, irritating but definitely interesting.

He had a sudden urge to take the glasses off and kiss her. Instead, he grinned.

"I worked out, so I had to take a shower. You wouldn't have wanted me to skip it."

She chuckled in spite of her pique. "No, I guess I wouldn't. But I *have* been worrying about whether I can find out everything I need to know before you have to leave this afternoon."

"What *I* can tell you won't take long," he said. "And after that you're on your own. Remember? That's why I hired you—because you're the expert."

They began a systematic survey of the display space, the items of the stock he had ordered and others that he planned to carry. He'd been right about himself as a source of information. Sabrina asked lots of questions he couldn't answer. She was beginning to get a basic grasp of what he wanted the store to be, but she'd have to do lots of research to learn how to accomplish that for him.

Finally they finished discussing the details of the section where they'd set up the hat department, and Sabrina leaned against its counter, surveying the entire store from that angle.

"I'll call Madge Howard tomorrow," she said, making a note on her pad. "She needs to get out here and get the decorating started as soon as these men are finished with the walls." She tapped her pencil thoughtfully. "I hope she doesn't want some of them repainted in a different color."

He stared at her. "A different color? What are you talking about?"

"Getting a decorator in here to do the interior. I've known Madge for years. She's expensive, but she's worth it. She does a great job."

"Forget that. We don't have money to pay *any* decorator, much less an expensive one. There's nothing at all in the budget for frivolous things like that."

"But Jarod, this isn't frivolous! It's absolutely essential! The right decor creates the right atmosphere in a store just as it does in a home. I intend to make this store something very special and I can't do that unless it's decorated well."

"It'll be special enough without all that. I'm not going to change the budget at this late date." He moved one hand in a gesture of finality. "Forget the decorator."

She took a deep breath, trying to restrain her anger. "You don't have that kind of control," she reminded him. "Not according to the terms we agreed on yesterday. Remember: we said that I can manage the funds available, subject to your final approval. You have to give me a chance to juggle the figures and see if I can take that amount from someplace else."

He scowled. "You can't. There's not a spare penny any place in the whole year's budget."

"Well, at least let me try to find some."

"I'm telling you, Sabrina, you don't need to hire somebody to decorate this place. Just hang a few of Angie's paintings around here and there—that'll be enough decorating."

His words finally soaked in through her thoughts of money and of Madge. She stared at him.

"Jarod!" she exclaimed. "What a super idea! We could not only display some of Angie's work, we could sell it for her! She really is a talented artist and she deserves to be seen!"

His frown dissipated. "*Now* you're talking! It'd be a little income for Angie, plus it'd be a push for all Indian arts and crafts." He began to pace back and forth. "There are some others I know who could use a few extra dollars, too," he said. "We could sell some of Sarah Talley's baskets, and my sister Darlene's husband's brother makes bows and arrows...."

Sabrina turned to a fresh sheet of paper and began to sketch. "Jarod, instead of just scattering all this haphazardly around the store, why don't we make a whole new department? An Indian arts and crafts department? We can be a cowboy and Indian store!"

She held out her crude drawing for his approval. "See? We could lay it out like this, over there in that corner!"

"Great! That'll be just great." He reached for the clipboard. "Here, let me just write down some more names as I think of them. I don't want to forget anybody."

He took her pencil, too, and began to write with quick, strong strokes. "I don't know these people's phone numbers, but you can look them up. Better yet, call Angie and let her do it. They'll be listed under Tahlequah and Stilwell..." He glanced up. "Of course, some of them won't have phones and..."

"Now, wait just a minute," she protested. "*I'll* find the artists and the merchandise. I'm the manager, remember?"

He stopped writing and looked up at her, surprised. "Yes, you're the manager," he said slowly. "Did someone say you weren't?"

"You just did."

"I did not. I'm just giving you a list . . ."

"I don't want a list," she interrupted. "I don't want to feel that I have to buy something from everyone whose name you write down just because that person is a friend or relative of yours. Who knows? I might not even like their work."

"I'm not telling you that you have to buy from every one of them," he shot back. "I'm just saying that if we carry Angie's work we need to consider these people, too." He smiled coldly. "And who knows?" he mimicked. "You might even like some of the things they do."

His eyes pierced hers, held them impaled. "You can't end up hurting a bunch of people's feelings, Sabrina," he said, weighting each word for emphasis. "Relationships are a whole lot more important than artistic judgments."

"Not when we're talking about the success or failure of this store," she retorted.

He threw the pencil onto the counter behind her. "Success!" he growled derisively. "What do they call it? The bitch goddess?"

"Maybe so, but what other reason is there for going into business? Why are you putting yourself through all this if you aren't in it for the money? It certainly isn't because you love to run a store...or as if you know how to run one!''

''Well, you don't know how to take orders,'' he snapped back at her. ''Remember, Sabrina, I'm hiring you...''

''Maybe you are,'' she corrected. ''And maybe you aren't. Not if I can do nothing but take orders from you. The contract we discussed says you're the owner, but you don't have all the control. If I'm going to be your manager, then I'm darn well going to be the manager. Those are the terms, and you can make your decision right now whether you want to keep me or not. If you don't, it's better to know now before we actually sign the papers and before I invest any more time and effort in this.''

He stared at her, silent, his eyes burning in the angled mask of his face.

She went on, her voice quieter, but full of a determination that showed she meant every word. ''Look, Jarod, if you're going to be so adamant about something like this, then what am I doing here? You told me that you aren't a businessman, that you wanted to hire me for my expertise. Well, then, let me use it. Don't dictate to me.''

His inscrutable black eyes held hers for a long moment. ''All right, then,'' he said at last. ''Find your own artists. But use some sense about how you do it.''

His tone hardened. ''Don't go down to Tahlequah and put an ad in the paper, or something, and then reject half the people who bring things to you.''

"Just how dumb do you think I am?" she retorted furiously.

"Dumb enough to think I was raised on a reservation," he snapped.

She gritted her teeth. Someday she'd get revenge for that remark, she vowed silently. But right now she wouldn't give him the satisfaction of knowing how angry it made her.

When she spoke again her tone was coolly professional. "I do need to get in touch with Angie while you're gone," she said. "I have no idea how to do that."

He nodded abruptly and growled as he scribbled on the notepad. "If she isn't there, Darlene can have her call you back."

He returned the clipboard, his eyes blazing down into hers for a second. Then he stalked away toward the offices and his apartment in the west wing of the building.

She stared after him, appalled at the way he'd left. How could they have been so close just yesterday and be so far apart right now? She'd never understand him, nor he her.

What was it, anyway, this mysterious element that was holding them together? Why hadn't one or both of them called off the whole arrangement during the fight they'd just had? They'd certainly been angry enough and far enough apart philosophically. Was he so determined to have a manager before he left town that he'd keep her no matter what?

And why had she stayed? There were certainly other ways she could be spending her time.

She looked back at his bold scrawl across the paper in her hand. It trembled a little before her eyes and her legs felt weak.

She walked around the counter and sat down on the stool behind it. How was she going to survive even a business relationship with him? She'd been on a roller coaster of rackingly fierce feelings ever since she'd met him, and now she felt it was moving faster than ever.

His heels striking the hard floor echoed across the big space. She looked up to see him returning, a cowboy hat on his head, his rigging bag in his hand.

"I'll be back in a few days," he said gruffly, not slowing on his way to the door. "We can sign the contracts then."

"All right."

"See you," he said abruptly. Then he was gone.

She watched the glass doors swing shut behind him. Then she returned back to the store, letting her eyes rove over the hundreds of square feet that she had to fill so soon with merchandise and people. What had she gotten herself into? Why was she risking her career to work for a man who had no business sense at all?

She ought to follow him right through those doors, she thought. She ought to get into her car and never come back.

But instead, she kept sitting there, not moving, not listening to the sounds of the workmen around her. She kept hearing Jarod's voice.

You'll end up hurting a bunch of people's feelings, he'd said. That was Jarod, the businessman.

Involuntarily she smiled. Well, she'd thought he was different from anyone she knew, and she'd been right. She'd certainly never heard a sentiment like that from any of her colleagues at Harwell and Neel's.

She doodled on the pad in front of her. Furious as Jarod's remark had made her at the time, it was intriguing. It really was an endearing attitude.

She saw that she was sketching Jarod's face, and stopped. Shaking back her hair she turned to her first page of notes.

They blurred in front of her, though, and a troublesome thought from the sleepless hours of the night before returned. Had her impulsive decision to stay in Tulsa subconsciously been based on her having met him?

She pushed back the stool and stood up. If that were true, she could never have been a bigger fool. The man was her complete opposite in every way.

Sabrina picked up the pad and pencil and began walking briskly toward the back of the store, smiling wryly to herself at the irony of that conclusion. She ought to call Martin and tell him that he'd been right on two counts. The idea of a relationship with Jarod was preposterous, and the announcement that she needed a big brother was absolutely true. In fact, what she needed was a keeper.

Chapter Five

But she and Martin went to dinner at the club as she'd promised, and she later talked to him twice on the phone without ever mentioning Jarod at all. She was so grateful for the respite from brotherly lecturing that she didn't want to bring up the subject, at least that was the excuse she gave herself.

However, a small honest part of her knew that the real reason she didn't want to talk about Jarod was the confusing ambivalence of her own feeling. For the first day after he'd left her so abruptly she'd managed to cling to a half-formed conviction that anything but a business relationship with him would be impossible; she'd since been possessed by an unquenchable desire to see him again.

She'd fought it with work, immersing herself in the store from early morning until long after midnight every day. Once she'd visited every other Western wear store in Tulsa and had begun looking at catalogs and reading widely about that segment of the retail business, she knew that lots of factors would determine whether or not they opened in just three weeks. There were some wonderful lines of exotic leather and appliquéd-cotton clothes that she wanted to carry, but it would take time to get the first shipments. And she wouldn't open without them. Sabrina was determined that the special quality she was creating for the store would be there from the very first day.

She talked to Madge Howard for hours about the atmosphere she wanted, then spent more hours poring over the budget and moving figures around. Finally she gave the budget to Zelda, the receptionist-secretary she'd hired, to retype, crossing her fingers that the maintenance for the year wouldn't require as much money as Jarod had originally allotted to it.

Back at her own desk, she looked over the columned printout one more time. Jarod would probably be furious with her.

Then she shrugged. If there were some sort of emergency, she'd simply take care of it with her own money.

The buzzer sounded as she refolded the paper. She pressed the button. "Your brother, Miss Dante," Zelda's voice announced.

"Send him in."

Martin appeared in her doorway. He was wearing his customary three-piece suit and buttoned-down shirt and carried his briefcase. She smiled at the image he made; he was always the epitome of the conservative businessman.

"Well, that was quick," she greeted him. "I call you in the morning, you arrive that very afternoon."

"Of course! I rushed right over because I can't wait to show you what great software I've invented for your accounting system," he bantered, coming in to sit in her wingback visitor's chair. "I want you to be pleased with the service we give."

"I'm sure I will," she said, matching his teasing tone. "It's certainly better than the service I'm getting from some of the hat and boot companies I've been calling. They all promise delivery sometime between Christmas and Easter."

She stood and began clearing away the piles of books and brochures that covered her desk. "You'd better go ahead and invent a software program for Indian and Southwestern art, too, so I can get rid of all these," she said. "We don't even have room here to spread out your instruction booklet." She glanced up at him in mock panic. "You did bring an instruction booklet, didn't you?"

He laughed. "For my sister, the computer idiot? I certainly did. It explains the whole system so clearly that a baby could use it."

She chuckled. "That still doesn't mean *I* could use it!"

He laughed, too. "Not to worry," he said soothingly.

He got up to help her transfer the piles of books to the credenza behind her desk. "Have you read all of this material?" he asked incredulously.

"I've not only read it, I've been trying to apply it," she said. "I've started a talent search—I need some promising new artists who are relatively unknown so I can stock our art department with good-quality work that won't be outrageously expensive."

"Are you having any luck?"

"Some. And I have a call in now to Jarod's niece to try to get some more leads."

Jarod's name hovered in the air for a moment, creating a small silence, then Martin put his briefcase on her desk and opened it.

"Let's go over the manual first," he suggested, "and then we'll put the disk into your machine and see what happens."

He had just begun his explanation when the phone rang and Zelda announced that it was Angie Fourkiller. Sabrina picked up the receiver.

"Angie? How are you?"

"Fine," came the soft-spoken answer. Then, after a pause, "My mom told me that you called."

"Yes. Your Uncle Jarod and I have decided to sell some Indian arts and crafts here in the store; and we'd like to start with a few of your paintings. Would you sell some of them to us?"

There was a long pause. "To sell to other people?"

"Yes. We'll take a percentage just as a gallery owner would do, but most of the money will be yours."

"Oh."

"We can decide on the exact prices when you bring me the paintings. And I'll talk to Jarod about the percentage on your work. He may want yours to be more than the others'."

"When will he be home?"

"I'm not really sure. When he left he just said he'd be back in a few days."

The girl didn't reply.

"Will that be all right with you?" Sabrina hesitated. "If we sell some of your paintings, I mean."

"I think so."

"Great. I'd like several if you have them—some of the miniatures that you had on display at the powwow, one or two of the medium-size ones, and I especially want *Triumphal Journey.*"

Angie was silent.

"Angie?"

"Yes?"

"Do you still have that one? Have you sold it to someone already?"

"No...I have it."

"Wonderful!"

Sabrina then asked her to recommend some other Indian artists. She then tried to set a date for delivery of Angie's work, but she was vague and noncommittal about both. Finally Sabrina told her that she had an appointment near Tahlequah on Wednesday and that she would come to see her then.

She hung up, frowning. "That was sort of strange," she commented, more to herself than to Martin. "I thought Angie would be really surprised and thrilled to have an outlet for her work, but she didn't seem to be."

"Maybe she's already hung in dozens of galleries," Martin joked. "You're probably tenth on the list."

"Maybe so." She toyed with her pencil, still thinking about the call. "And I'm disappointed about the referrals. I really expected her to give me some names of people I'd like."

"I'm sorry," Martin commiserated. He waited for a minute, then he picked up the manual again. "Not to rush you, little sister, but we do have a lot to cover here..."

"Of course! I'm sorry. Let's get right back to work."

When they'd gone over the whole system and Martin had answered all her questions, Sabrina got up to make a fresh pot of coffee. "Stay and visit for a while," she suggested. "I've got to have a break before I think about another number or another piece of merchandise."

"That sounds great. I'm going straight from here to the computer show at the Civic Center. Then after that is a dinner date with a representative of a company in Dallas. I won't even get a chance to run this evening."

"Then it'll all be worth it," she teased. "I'd work all day *and* night to keep from having to run."

He shook his head in mock concern. "And it shows, too. Just look what terrible shape you're in!"

She made a face at him and switched on the coffee maker.

"Speaking of running," he said, "one of my running buddies, Ron Shelton, is having a party at his house next weekend. I'd mentioned that you're back in town and he asked me to invite you. I told him you'd probably come."

"But I probably won't," she retorted. She spread her hands in a gesture of helplessness. "Look, Martin, you know how completely snowed under I am. Right now, a party would just be a complete waste of time."

"You can't work *all* the time."

"Well, even if I did have time to go out, I wouldn't want to go to a runners' party," she declared. "I don't have a thing in common with crazy people who get up at all hours of the day and night to go out and run their hearts out in all kinds of weather up and down the streets of Tulsa, ruining their knees and their backs, and no doubt damaging their hearts and lungs as well. I'd have nothing to talk to them about, and I'd be bored stiff!"

She was breathless by the time she came to the end of her diatribe and they were both laughing.

"*Now* who's doing the stereotyping?" he demanded.

Then he sobered. "But you should come with me anyway, Sabrina. You need to start getting back into circulation, back in your own social circles."

She slanted a knowing glance at him. So he *hadn't* stopped worrying about her and Jarod! He'd just been waiting for the right moment to mention it again.

"Thanks, Martin, but I can choose my own friends." She gave him her best smile. "Really I can. Don't worry."

"How can I keep from worrying?" he asked. "You're dating this guy you hardly know, you're working for him; soon your whole life will be tangled up with him."

He was slipping back into his big-brotherly tone. She sighed. She was too tired and too harried to take another lecture right now.

"Martin, I'm working for Jarod, but that's it. I've decided that a personal relationship with him would be really unwise."

The look of relief that came over his face filled her with guilt. Where had that reassurance come from? Had she truly made that decision? Well, she'd know when she saw Jarod again, she thought.

She racked her brain for something else to talk about. "Oh, yes," she said. "I looked at a couple of condos this week. I think I'm going to buy at Utica Oaks."

He looked startled.

"Oh, Martin, do you think it's too soon to leave Mother alone?" she asked worriedly. "I was afraid of that."

"No," he answered quickly. "I wasn't thinking that at all. I was just wondering how you could work in looking at real estate this week on top of everything else you've been doing."

"I could do it because I'm a veritable powerhouse of energy," she said lightly. "I never eat, I never sleep." Then she grew serious. "It didn't take a lot of time; I pretty well knew what I wanted and where."

She played with her pencil again, frowning thoughtfully. "I guess I decided I had to move out when I called San Francisco on Monday. I actually quit my job instead of taking a leave of absence the way I'd planned, and it gave me a weird feeling that I was burning all my bridges. Suddenly I felt this urgent need to have my very own place again—I need to have one thing that feels permanent in the midst of all the changes."

He nodded. "I understand. And don't worry about Mother. It'll probably be easier for her to let you go now than it would be later."

"I think so, too." She looked up at him. "Thanks, Martin. I'm relieved that you agree."

"And I'm glad that *you* agree with *me* about Redfeather," he replied. "Now all I have to do is get you to Ron's party, introduce you to some suitable men and my brotherly duty is done!"

"No chance," she told him, laughing. "That you'll never do." She glanced at her watch and stood up. "I don't want to rush you, Martin, but break time is over. I, for one, have to get back to work."

Only after he'd gone did she allow herself to think of his last remark about Jarod. He'd been so trust-

ingly happy that just remembering it made her cringe.
Oh, *why* had she lied to him?

Or had she?

The end of Sabrina's first week on the job proved to
be just as hectic as the beginning, and the second week
was worse. She began going in even earlier to interview prospective employees and staying later to check
their references and begin their training. Beside her,
Jarod had hired only one worker, a friend of his
named Lawrence Walkingstick, who was stocker and
all-around handyman. She had to find everyone else
from Zelda, her secretary, to Dorothy, her assistant;
twenty-five clerks; a window dresser and two custo-
dians.

Tuesday afternoon Sabrina was hurriedly sifting
through a new stack of applications when Zelda
buzzed her. "It's Mr. Redfeather," she said. "He's at
the airport and he's looking for Lawrence. Do you
know where he is?"

Her pulse leaped crazily. "Yes. I'll talk to him,
Zelda."

"Yes, ma'am."

"Hello? Sabrina?" His rich drawl slowed her
heartbeat painfully.

She swallowed. "Hello, Jarod."

"I left my truck here at the airport, but the darn
thing won't start. Could you send Lawrence out to
pick me up?"

"He isn't here; he had to go to Tahlequah." She
held on to the receiver as if it were a lifeline. "But I

can come. I'm just getting ready to go out on an errand anyway."

"Great. I'll be downstairs near the American Airlines counter."

"I'm leaving right now."

She saw him the minute she pulled up at the curb; he was pacing back and forth, watching for her. His big form seemed to fill the whole section of the car window; the sense of tightly drawn energy that she'd felt in him at their first meeting was in every movement he made. Their eyes met and held.

She got out to open the trunk and he reached her just as she turned away from it. His smile was instantaneous, a magnet to draw her to him. He opened his arms instinctively, as if they'd been lovers for years. She walked into them.

That one second erased the days they'd been apart. The exhaustion that had been building in her drained away into the warm solid strength of his touch. She clung to him.

The differences between them disappeared and she forgot the way they had parted. She needed him so much, she knew, although it wasn't a conscious thought. She needed him and she wanted him to kiss her.

But his lips brushed her hair. "How've you been, beautiful Sabrina?"

The tenderness in his tone destroyed her; she never wanted to leave the warm circle of his arms. "All right," she murmured.

She looked up at him. "How about you?"

"Battered and bruised," he said dryly, keeping one arm around her as he threw his rigging bag into the car. "I've had a week of rotten rides I don't want to talk about."

They got into the car and she started the motor, "Do we need to do anything about the truck before we go?" she asked.

"No. I called that filling station on the corner near the store and they're sending somebody out to get it— I'll walk over and pick it up there late this afternoon."

He tossed his hat onto the back seat, then winced, rubbing his shoulder. "I just didn't want to wait here for them to fix it," he explained. "I want to hit a hot shower and try to steam out some of these aches and pains."

She threw him a worried glance over her shoulder as she worked the car out into the stream of traffic. "Oh, maybe I should take you back to the store first. I'm supposed to meet the real estate agent at my new condo at three o'clock to sign the closing papers; I'd thought we could drop by there on our way."

"You've bought a condo? On top of all the work you've been turning out? Busy lady."

She smiled. "You sound just like my brother." *I'll have to tell Martin that,* she thought wryly. *He'll love it that he and Jarod do have something in common.*

He made a dismissive gesture. "The shower can wait," he said. "I'll go with you. Don't make an extra trip."

As they began the drive across town she gave him a report on the employees she'd hired so far and on the stock she'd ordered. He relaxed into the seat, his head leaning back against the headrest but he listened carefully, interjecting an occasional question.

"Anybody else from Tahlequah except Lawrence?" he asked. "I told several people to come on up and apply if they wanted..."

He interrupted himself and sat up straight when she pulled off Twenty-first Street into the entrance of an exclusive high-rise condominium. She identified herself to the guard and the spiked iron gated swung inward.

"Is *this* your new condo?"

"Yes. I want a place of my own, but I didn't want to go too far from the old neighborhood."

He grinned wryly and shook his head. "You must have forgotten to tell me that among your many activities this week you gave yourself a raise. Somehow I get the feeling that the amount I originally quoted as your salary won't be quite enough to pay the rent on this place."

The words carried an undertone she couldn't quite identify, and Sabrina remembered his remarks about the opulence of her mother's house. The emotion in his voice wasn't jealousy, she mused as they caught the elevator in the luxurious lobby. It was more complicated than that. She tried to put a name to it but couldn't; he said nothing more.

The agent and the building manager let them into the top-floor condominium. Sabrina invited Jarod to walk through and look at it while she read and signed the papers the two men had ready for her. He came back into the living room just as they finished and he walked with them down the hallway and into the kitchen.

"Most of the changes I want will be in here," Sabrina said to the manager. "We'll be replacing the cabinets with glass-doored oak ones and I want an island work space in the center. I'm covering it with Quimper tile and we'll use that on all the other counter tops as well."

"That'll be fine, Ms. Dante."

She ran her hand over the surface of the counter. "I hope *this* tile won't be too hard to remove. The workmen are supposed to start immediately, but I know that no matter what, it's going to take longer than I'd like—these things always do, don't they?"

She turned to include Jarod in her smile, but he didn't smile back. He was running one hand over the tile counter top, as she had done, and his eyes were fixed on her, their black depths blazing. She stared back, trying to read them, and suddenly she had that same feeling she'd had before, the sensation that he was judging her. Why? What in the world was he thinking?

Then she realized that the manager was talking to her. "Who will be overseeing this work for you, Ms. Dante?"

"Madge Howard. We've already made the necessary selections and she tells me that she and the workmen will be here on Thursday morning."

"Fine. I'll be expecting them."

Soon after that the manager and the agent left and she turned to Jarod. "Well? What do you think?"

"I think it's fine," he said forcefully. "I think it's luxurious. And beautiful. And extravagant." He paced the length of the room to stand in front of the wall of glass in the breakfast area.

"Extravagant?"

"You bet. Before you even change anything. Before you rip off the top of the counters and build islands in the middle of the floor and all that nonsense." He swung around to face her. "Sabrina, this place is good enough for anybody," he grated. "Just the way it is."

Dumbfounded, she stared at him. "Well, I don't see anything wrong with having it the way I want it," she said defensively. "After all, I'm willing to pay for it."

"Maybe so," he retorted, "but there is such a thing as being sinfully wasteful."

"That's a matter of opinion. You have no right to judge me."

"You asked me what I thought, and I told you." He turned away angrily and went back toward the living room.

She followed, furious. "We'd better be getting back to work," she said coldly. "I'm sorry I took up your time with my little domestic details."

He jerked the door open and held it while she went to get the key the manager had left. He was completely silent, but the argument continued to simmer inside her all the way down to the car. What was it to him, anyway? What did he care what her life-style was? What was it to him how much money she spent?

First it was her mother's house that was too... different, and now hers was extravagant. Different from things down on the reservation, he'd said.

Out of the blue she remembered his remark about the Indian artists and craftsmen. "There are some others I know who could use a few extra dollars." The words echoed in her head and she saw the contrast between her condominium and his rustic cabin.

They arrived at the car, still mute. When they were settled inside, she faced him.

"At least I'm making jobs for people," she said stiffly. "You have to admit that."

His eyes flashed to hers, surprised. An involuntary smile slowly curved his lips. "True," he said dryly. "I do have to admit that."

His eyes wouldn't let hers go. The smile faded, but it didn't disappear entirely.

She gave him a tentative smile in return and felt the antagonism between them begin to melt away.

Finally he shrugged. "Spend your money any way you want to," he said diffidently. "It really *isn't* any of my business. But watch that kind of extravagance at the store, okay?"

She winced inside, thinking of the budget changes she'd already made, the decorating she'd commissioned. She concentrated on firing up the ignition, letting her hair fall across her face to hide her thoughts, dreading the moment she'd have to tell him.

Well, what she'd done was within the terms of her contract, she thought as she drove toward the gate. He'd hired her; he'd just have to live with the decisions she made.

They talked in a desultory way as they drove to the store, but they kept to safely neutral topics. She could feel his scrutiny, unobtrusive as it was, and she had the same sensation that she'd had that afternoon on the way to Tsa-La-Gi: he was sizing her up, measuring her against some invisible standard.

When they arrived at the store, she parked the car and turned to look at him, resentful of his silent study. Well, how did I do? she wanted to ask. Did I pass whatever test this is?

They got out of the car and went to the trunk for his hat and bag. He was holding his shoulder more stiffly than ever.

"Look, I'd like to head straight for that shower," he said. "Let's wait and get down to the business details over dinner."

She hesitated, surprised. One minute he was lambasting her for being sinfully wasteful, the next he was giving her some kind of secret examination, and now he was assuming as a matter of course that they'd have dinner together.

"Oh, I don't know," she said. "Going to a restaurant would probably be too extravagant." She slanted a challenging glance up at him. "I'm not in the mood to cook, and I really think you're too tired to do it."

He gave her a long, straight look from beneath his black eyebrows. Finally he grinned. "No fair," he said. "I've already apologized."

"I don't remember your saying, 'I'm sorry.'"

"I said it was none of my business," he replied, putting his hand on her back to escort her into the building. "Isn't that the same thing?"

His touch was like fire. It dissolved all her resentment and recreated the thrill, the warmth, of being in his arms.

"I want to clean up and maybe grab a little nap," he was saying. "How about if I pick you up around eight?"

"No," she said quickly, in one last attempt to cling to the fantasy that she might be his business associate and nothing more. "I'll meet you. Where do you want to go?"

"How about Chi-Chi's?"

"Fine. I'll be there at eight."

She went into her office and closed the door between them, an instinctive gesture of self-protection.

But she knew it was a futile one. She *had* lied to Martin. If she could walk into Jarod's arms without even thinking about it and long to stay there, then within the same hour be searching his face for a shred of a clue about his feelings for her; if a few angry remarks from him could make her question the way she'd lived all her life; if a couple of minutes of thoughtful observation from him could make her despair of knowing what he was thinking, then she *was* involved in a personal relationship with him.

It was already too late.

Chapter Six

Jarod was waiting for her just inside the bar. When he saw her come in he pushed his glass away and stood up, moved by the same sudden impulse that had made him take her into his arms when they met that afternoon. She looked small and fragile in the crowd that filled the restaurant's entry; delicate and a little bit lost. She should be in his arms where she belonged.

But not for long. He shook his head in disgust for even putting himself into this one more social situation with her. She belonged in that quarter-million dollar condominium that she was ripping the guts out of, not in a log cabin down in the Cookson Hills.

He came out of the bar and moved toward her with that smooth, rolling cowboy's walk of his. She couldn't take her eyes away. It was a predator's walk, completely sure, entirely certain.

"Hello, Sabrina."

"Have you been waiting long?"

"Maybe twenty minutes."

"I'm sorry."

"No problem."

They watched each other's faces, exchanging different messages with their eyes than with their words, standing very close together until the hostess came to seat them. They were almost touching, but not quite.

Then he took her elbow as the young woman led them down a step to the main dining room; and the old thrill flooded through her. She knew then that she wanted his touch again far more than she wanted food or talk.

However, he let her go when they got to the table, and the waiters hovered over them with chips and salsa, nachos and sangria. He turned the conversation firmly to the subject of the store, and they discussed the projected timetable for the opening and talked in detail about the orders of saddle blankets and other tack. They decided how many more clerks to hire and agreed that Lawrence Walkingstick could handle much more responsibility than he'd originally been given.

She watched his face as they spoke, wishing she could turn the conversation to him, longing to know what he was thinking and feeling about her. She'd expected this to be more a date than a business meeting in spite of all the catching up they had to do, but evidently she'd been wrong.

Over the steaming enchiladas and chimichangas she told him amusing stories about her visits to their competitors, and they listed the ways in which the store, Jarod Redfeather, would be uniquely different. They were lingering over the fried ice cream and coffee when she finally asked, "Are you going to tell me how you hurt your shoulder? Your hot shower seems to have helped, but I can tell that it still hurts."

He shrugged, then winced when the movement hurt him. "I suppose I might as well admit how stupid I was," he said, smiling. "I drew this crazy bull named Aztec..."

She smiled back at him, then glanced toward the entrance. Her cup froze to her lips. It couldn't be!

Three men followed the hostess down the steps into the dining area and she saw that indeed it was. Martin and two of his friends were going to pass right by their table.

Quickly she looked away, hoping that he hadn't seen her. There was nothing she'd hate more tomorrow morning than trying to explain to Martin why she'd gone out with Jarod after making that brave declaration of independence.

"What's wrong?" Jarod asked.

"What? Oh...nothing." She moved her chair slightly so that she was facing away from the aisle.

"Please finish your story," she said, leaning toward him across the table. Martin and his friends were almost even with them now; if she could just blend into the scenery until they were safely past . . .

"Sabrina!"

She stiffened. There was no way she could escape.

Jarod's eyes were on her face; she turned away from his searching look to meet her brother's.

"Martin!" she exclaimed, hoping that she sounded sincerely surprised.

There was a general chorus of greetings and introductions—one of the men with Martin was his runner friend, Ron Shelton, the other was an old family friend, James Anderson. When Jarod turned to shake hands with them, Martin flashed her a dismayed look.

Then Ron was talking to her. "Martin says he invited you to my party, but has he remembered to tell you it'll be at Arrowhead? The guest list sort of snowballed and I thought the club would be more comfortable than my house." He gave her a charming smile, then swung around to include Jarod. "Please come, too, if you can. It's tomorrow night."

"Thanks," Jarod replied abruptly. "I'm busy."

They visited for a few minutes, teasing Sabrina about running and welcoming her back to town. But she had trouble responding: Jarod was morosely silent, and Martin silently questioned her every time their eyes met. After what seemed an age to her they moved on to their own table.

As soon as they'd gone, Jarod dropped his napkin onto the table and signaled for the check. "I've got to be going."

She stared at him. "But you haven't finished your ice cream," she protested. "Or your story. I want to hear the end of it . . ."

"Later," he interrupted gruffly. "I want to run a couple of miles tonight. I didn't have a chance to this morning."

The waiter brought the check and Jarod dropped several bills on it. He stood up and pushed back his chair, then came around to hers.

They threaded their way out of the dining room and across the foyer without talking at all. Outside, he stopped on the walk that led to the parking area.

"Where's your car?"

"Over there."

"I'll see you to it."

"Thank you."

She glanced up at his set face as they went toward the car, determined to breach the wall of ice that had dropped between them. "I thought Martin's friend's party sounded like fun," she said, grasping the first topic that popped into her head. "You'd probably enjoy it; the talk will be all physical fitness and athletics. Would you like to go?"

"Hell, no," he said savagely. "I've never been one to hang out at country clubs and it's too late to start now."

"Jarod!"

"What?"

"What's happened all of a sudden? What's wrong? Why are you acting this way?"

"I'm not acting," he growled stubbornly, holding out his hand for her keys. "What you see here is the real Jarod Redfeather."

He unlocked the car and held the door for her. "Good night, Sabrina," he said abruptly. "See you tomorrow at the store."

He gave her the keys and she watched him stride toward his pickup truck. Then she jerked the ignition on and gunned the motor.

All right, she thought furiously. If that was the way he wanted to be, that was perfectly all right with her. This was the perfect incident to make her get off that roller-coaster ride of extreme emotions he'd taken her on since the minute they'd met. It was too steep a drop from its highs to its lows; she was sick of it.

But she paced the balcony outside her room until the wee hours of the morning, mystified and angry. Was it an Indian trait to swing from one intense mood to another?

Was it really true that Indians were stoics who never talked about their feelings? Jarod certainly didn't. He wouldn't if she put a gun to his head.

She thought about the times she'd so desperately wanted him to talk to her. When she'd broken off their lovemaking at his cabin, he'd cut her off with sarcasm as she tried to discuss her reasons.

And then when he'd told her he wanted to see her again, he'd done it not with words, but with the offer of a job.

Or maybe she'd misunderstood the message, she thought bitterly. Maybe all he'd ever wanted was a manager for his store.

She went to her room and got into bed, but couldn't sleep. For the dozenth time she relived every moment of the evening, searching for the reason Jarod had suddenly become so inexplicably cold. After she'd introduced him to Martin...

Martin! That was another problem. He'd never believe her again when she said she wasn't personally involved with Jarod.

She managed a bitter smile as she finally closed her eyes. What an irony! This time she'd be telling the truth.

She woke from a fitful sleep just before dawn. Her first thoughts were incoherent reflections of her dreams, and for a little while she lay looking out at the night, trying to unravel the skein of tangled emotions that had awakened her. Finally she got up and went to run her tub—there was no way she could go back to sleep and she certainly wasn't going to just lie there and think.

While she soaked in the fragrant, hot bath she forced her mind onto the day to come. She'd go in to the store as soon as she was dressed, she decided. That would keep her mind busy and maybe she could select the last group of interviewees from the stack of applications on her desk. This was the day she was going to Tahlequah and she needed to use every minute.

She concentrated on what she wanted to accomplish and kept the thoughts of Jarod at bay until she pulled into her parking spot near the door of the store's west wing. His pickup was there, parked across from Lawrence Walkingstick's, and the image of him striding angrily toward it at Chi-Chi's flashed across her mind. She stepped on her parking brake and flung open her door. She didn't even want to see him today; she wasn't strong enough right now to have him jerk her emotions around as if she were his puppet.

She let herself into the peaceful dimness of the building and went straight to her office. Jarod, evidently, was still asleep and Lawrence was probably at the restaurant next door having breakfast.

She made coffee, then sat down in front of the applications and started reading the top one. She'd hurry and be ready to leave as soon as Zelda arrived.

She'd just finished her first cup of coffee and had chosen two people she definitely wanted to see when there was a knock at the door. Startled, she glanced at her watch. Probably Lawrence was back and ready to report on the stock that had arrived yesterday.

"Come in."

It was Jarod.

"Good morning," he said brusquely.

"Good morning."

Without waiting to be invited, he came in and went straight to the coffee maker, poured himself a cup, then turned a straight chair by the side of her desk and straddled it. She watched him take a sip of coffee and set the mug on her desk.

"Why don't you come and join me for a cup of coffee?" she asked.

The mild sarcasm elicited a slight smile. "Thanks."

She was furious with herself; his being so close was making her hands tremble. She couldn't stop looking at him. He was wearing an old gray jogging suit and a rolled red bandanna for a sweatband; they were the perfect foils for his powerful frame and the fascinating angles of his face.

She tore her eyes away and forced herself to get up and move. "Did you decide to do your jogging this morning instead of last night?" she asked as she refilled her cup.

"Both." He watched her come back to the desk. "On my way back in just now I saw your car and realized that we didn't get around to talking last night about the arts and crafts."

And that's not all we didn't talk about, she thought. She stared at him.

Finally she said coolly, "Well, I really don't have time to get into it now. I'm just going to finish choosing the last group of people I want to interview, then I'm leaving for Tahlequah. I'll probably be down there the rest of the day; I have an appointment with a beadworker named Molly Bear, and I'm going by Angie's to pick up some of her paintings."

"How'd you make an appointment with Molly?" he asked curiously.

"What do you mean? On the phone, of course. Does she usually not answer it or something?"

"Did you talk to her?"

"N-o-o," she said slowly, thinking back to the call she'd made. "I talked with her sister. She said Molly was working. She checked with her, though, and came back to the phone to say that today around eleven would be fine."

He shrugged. "Well, you may have a problem or two there."

"*What* are you talking about?" she demanded.

"When Molly answers the phone, it's in Cherokee. She doesn't speak any English."

"Oh, no!" Sabrina wailed. Then she brightened. "Maybe her sister can translate. Does she live with her, perhaps?"

"Sort of. But she works in Tulsa. She's only with Molly on weekends."

Sabrina nodded. "It was last Saturday morning that I called."

Nervously she pushed the stack of papers away from her. "This is awful!" she exclaimed. "Why didn't she tell me that? I *have* to see her today because I want to commission her to make some of those beaded suede dresses she's famous for. It'll take some time for her to finish them, and I want at least one to show when we have our grand opening."

He shrugged and picked up the mug again. "Everybody knows she doesn't speak English; she probably thought you'd bring an interpreter with you. You'll need to pick one up someplace."

"I know!" she cried. "But where? Who would be willing to go with me on such short notice? Where do you just pick up somebody who speaks Cherokee?"

He took another sip of coffee, his eyes on hers in a level gaze. "Right here."

"You?"

"Yeah. I want to talk to Ridge anyway."

Excitement and gladness winged through her first, then dismay. She *couldn't* spend all day with him!

She tried to think of a graceful way to say that, then she realized that she couldn't afford to give in to her emotional turmoil. He was her only chance to talk to Molly.

Just keep it business, Sabrina, she told herself. Keep it all business and get some things accomplished.

"Fine," she said. "Thank you. We can get you caught up on the arts and crafts while we drive."

He nodded briskly. "You finish up whatever you're doing here and I'll shower. We can be on the road by nine."

The June morning was warm but it was nothing like the heat of late afternoon, and they drove with the windows open to the summer countryside. It seemed to her that their talk and even the push of her emotions slowed to fit its rhythm.

"Have you known Molly Bear for a long time?"

"For as long as I can remember."

"It's fascinating to think that she never learned English. Did she ever go to school?"

"That I don't know. But I didn't say she never learned English."

She turned to him, amazed, feeling that she'd been tricked. "You did! You said . . ."

"I said she *speaks* nothing but Cherokee. My guess would be that she understands quite a lot of English."

Silently, she absorbed that. "She sounds like a real character. This could be an interesting trip."

"It could be," he agreed, and the sexy tone of his voice carried a double meaning. She looked at him more closely. He met her eyes and smiled, a strange combination of a question and a statement in his level gaze.

They passed the graveled turnoff to his place and the memories that came back to her made her fall silent. They took the next side road and drove for what seemed to be miles up its narrow track. It was rutted and rocky, and Sabrina felt that she'd had a real wilderness experience by the time they'd jolted to the top of a ridge and then down into a wooded valley where a modest gray brick house was the only habitation.

"It seems so remote!" she exclaimed. "No wonder Molly doesn't speak any English—she may not even speak Cherokee anymore, either. She probably never sees anyone to talk to in any language!"

He chuckled. "This is only four miles or so from my cabin as the crow flies. It's practically the heart of civilization."

"That all depends on your definition of civilization," she declared as he parked the truck in the bare, packed-earth yard. "I say it's a miracle they ever got enough bricks in here to build a house!"

"Just trust the Bureau of Indian Affairs," he said as they crossed the yard. "They've built houses just like this all over these hills. Evidently they don't have a whole lot of plans and colors to pick from.''

He knocked at the open door and called out in Cherokee.

A moment later a rotund, middle-aged woman appeared. She welcomed Jarod warmly with a smile and such a spate of Cherokee that Sabrina wished fervently that she could understand them, then moved back and gestured for them to enter.

Sabrina gasped when she stepped into the room; it was a direct contrast to the bland, white-man's exterior of the house. Everything in it was very interesting and very Indian.

The sheer color that it held was a delight; the walls were hung with buckskin beaded in rich reds and blues; containers of bright glass beads and matching ribbons were everywhere. Scattered over the tables and the seats of the couch were hair ornaments and belts, their intricate designs in various stages of completion. On the back of one chair was a suede dress, its beaded yoke almost completed.

Openly fascinated, Sabrina wandered from one item to another, exclaiming over the originality of the designs and the quality of the work. Jarod and Molly were settled on the couch, visiting happily.

Finally Jarod indicated that the amenities were concluded and asked what Sabrina would like him to say. She had him explain about the store and her desire to show off the beaded dresses during the grand opening celebration.

Molly's first reply was an unequivocal "no," but Sabrina refused to accept that. She had Jarod tell her that she must have not one, but two of the dresses because she wanted to wear one herself for the grand opening and still have one to display in the center of the store.

Molly's round face folded into a small, pleased grin. She voiced a few more objections, but Sabrina overcame them, and at last Molly agreed to sell them the almost-completed dress she had on hand and to do another as soon as possible.

Jarod flashed Sabrina a look that was both surprised and admiring.

That changed to astonishment when, after a bit of bargaining, Molly agreed to think about doing two more. She wouldn't talk about a specific date to set as a deadline for them, though, and finally Jarod explained to Sabrina that they could do nothing more to persuade her. Sabrina would have to be satisfied with the indefinite promise that Molly would deliver the dresses "when the trees show their colors."

Then Sabrina had Jarod ask her the prices of some of the smaller items she had on hand. At first again her answer was "no."

She didn't want to sell so much that she'd have nothing to take to the courthouse lawn on Saturdays, Jarod translated.

"The People gather at the courthouse square in Tahlequah for an informal trade fair every week," he explained. "It's been a tradition ever since Removal."

"Oh," Sabrina replied. "Then you must take a vacation. Just sell everything to me and you won't have to carry it to town or sit and watch it. You can wander around and talk to all your friends!"

This elicited a dry chuckle from Molly, and in a little while she gestured that Sabrina could take some of the items she liked. As she began wrapping them, Jarod smiled at Sabrina and gave a silent little sign of victory.

The twinkling sense of fun that she loved was back in his eyes again and it made her knees go weak. He had the same look he'd had at the powwow when showing her the sensual dance that he'd just made up; that same glint had been in his eye when he'd taken her home to see his breechclout-and-feather collection. *This* Jarod she couldn't resist.

They worked out the details of price and Sabrina wrote Molly a check. By the time they told her goodbye, Sabrina felt as if she didn't even need an interpreter; there was a real rapport between them now.

"Well, I'd put my money on you in any trade, any time," Jarod told her on the way to the truck. "You've missed your calling. I want to set you up in the horse trading business."

She laughed, loving the admiration in his voice.

"Well, you may have helped a little. After all, an honest interpreter's the key to this kind of a deal."

"We do make a pretty good team, don't we?"

The words wrapped her in warmth. His eyes held hers. For a minute after they reached the truck, neither one of them moved to part.

Finally he opened the door and she got in, trying to regain her equilibrium.

"I guess we'd better pick up Angie's paintings and then head back," she said, waving a last goodbye to Molly through the rear window. "We should be able to get to the store long before it gets too late in the day."

He slanted a thoughtful glance at her as he put the truck into reverse and swung it around. "Oh, I don't know," he drawled. "It's an awfully pretty day to spend inside. Seems to me we ought to be looking for a swimming hole somewhere to jump into."

She laughed. "Well, that's a switch. Here I am, the gung-ho, loyal employee trying my best to get back to work and my lazy boss is encouraging me to play hooky."

"You deserve to. You've heard the saying about all work and no play..."

"Oh?" She pretended to be very indignant. "So now you're telling me that I'm dull? Is that what you're saying?"

He laughed, too, and the warm, rich sound was as unsettling as his smile. "No, it isn't." He looked at her. "That's not what I'm saying at all."

She glanced away from the temptation in his eyes and the seduction in his tone. "You could've fooled me," she said quickly.

A short time later he took a fork in the graveled road instead of going back to the highway. It was a minute before she noticed.

"Hey, where are we going?" she asked. "Are you really serious about running away from your responsibilities?"

"But I'm not running away from them," he protested, "I'm going by to see my grandfather and to check on my horses. Wouldn't you say that both of those are responsible things for me to be doing?"

"You're hopeless!" she exclaimed, laughing. "I'm beginning to see that there's no way I can win in this conversation."

He flashed her that look again. "Right. So you might as well just relax and enjoy."

The words echoed in the silence between them. I want to, she admitted silently, her defenses crumbling away. That's exactly what I want to do.

The indolent sounds of the insects and the faint rustle of a breeze in the trees that enclosed the road seemed to magnify her thoughts. It was getting harder and harder to remember why she'd been in such a hurry, and more difficult to think about anything but Jarod.

They stopped at a tiny house in the next valley, but Ridge wasn't at home.

Jarod speculated that he might be cutting through the woods to Molly's. "We've probably just missed him," he said. "He usually drops in on her every day; they talk awhile and smoke a couple of pipes together."

"So that's why she wouldn't set a deadline for the dresses: she doesn't know how much of her time Ridge is going to take!"

He chuckled. "She wouldn't set a deadline because she isn't going to be bound by dates and clocks," he said. "I think it's in our blood to hate that."

"Well, maybe my Cherokee blood is coming to the fore," she said, surprised to hear the words actually coming from her mouth. "I'm beginning not to care whether I go back to work today or not."

"Atta girl! You'll be wearing buckskin and beads before you know it."

"I will if your grandfather will help Molly instead of hindering her!" she exclaimed. "And I think you ought to tell him that!"

They were laughing at the vision of Ridge sewing beads on dresses when they pulled up at Jarod's cabin.

They were bantering back and forth as they got out and started along the walk to the front of the house. It sat, ensconced on top of its bluff in the sunlight, the chairs on the old-fashioned porch overlooking the river below. The air was warm and heavy with the sounds and scents of summer. This was a world unto itself—there was no need for anything else.

"I love this place," she said, the words bursting out of her on the force of the pure joy she felt. "Whoever built it has absolutely fabulous taste."

"I had fabulous foresight, too," he declared. "I built it on this spot so I wouldn't have a long walk to the river; on hot days like this I just dive off the bluff and into the water!"

He took her hand. "Come on over here and join me." He pulled her toward the bluff.

"Jarod! What are you doing?"

He eyed her innocently as he slipped an arm around her waist. "We are going swimming, aren't we?"

"We can't, we aren't dressed for it," she protested, laughing helplessly.

He pulled her closer to the edge.

She resisted, trying to dig her flat sandals into the ground. "You may be Butch Cassidy, but I'm not exactly the Sundance Kid," she said through the laughter bubbling up in her throat. "Don't you know the fall would kill us?"

She twisted in the circle of his arm and eyed the path that was worn down the side of the cliff, moving them closer to it.

"The water does look good, though," she said panting through her giggles. "Why don't we go down to it this way?"

With a sudden effort she escaped his arm, and grabbing his hand she began to run down the steep incline, pulling him after her, both of them giggling and shouting like children on a holiday.

"You're the one who's going to get thrown in the river," he threatened as they raced off the path and onto the rocky edge of the shore. "And if you make me get these boots wet, I'll hold you under."

He stopped to struggle out of a high-topped boot, holding her off with one hand, but before he could remove the other one, she took advantage of his one-legged stance and pulled him off balance into the cool water.

"I warned you!" he roared. "You're gonna pay for this!"

He caught her wrist and dragged her into his arms, rolling with her farther into the shallow water near the riverbank until both of them were soaked to the skin. A shimmering delight darted through her, a mingling of wild happiness and intense desire.

Her eyes still teasingly defiant, full of laughter and growing passion, she gasped. "I thought you said you'd hold me under. Let's see you do it, cowboy."

Their mirthful faces were only inches apart, and he answered the reckless challenge by catching her lips with his, taking them into his fierce possession with all his strength. He held her head cupped in his hand while he captured her mouth with his, so rough and wild in his hunger that it took away her breath.

Finally he tore his lips away. "I've decided I'd rather just hold you," he murmured huskily, his eyes devouring her.

Sabrina watched the laughter in his face melt into desire before she closed her eyes and gave herself up to the sweetly slow insistence of a new kiss. She trembled and made a little cry of pleasure deep in her throat at the sharp provocation of it, at the thrill of their lips parting at the same instant to find the piercing pleasure of the other's stroking tongue.

He plundered the warm depths of her mouth with a relentless determination, pressing her wet body ever closer to him; she led him on with her hands, with her tongue and with the wordless moans of pleasure that escaped her.

At last they pulled apart, trembling with the passion of their kiss. One of his hands was at her waist, holding her motionless. The other touched the wet skin of the nape of her neck and lifted her streaming mass of hair. His eyes clung to her face.

Then he looked down at her heaving breasts, the nipples peaking hard and firm through the soaking fabric of her blouse.

"We'd better get to the house and get out of these wet clothes," he muttered hoarsely. "They're getting in my way."

"I tried to help," she murmured, willing the pounding of her heart to slow down. "I got one boot off for you."

"I'm glad you mentioned that," he drawled sternly, leading her toward shore. "I warned you not to get my boots wet. Now you're going to carry this one to the house and saddle-soap both of them as soon as they're dry."

"We'll see," she teased, pulling back. "But we can't go now. I thought you wanted to go for a swim."

His eyes found hers and grew even darker, smoldering with a passion denied for the last time. "I want you," he growled.

He stood and pulled her up into his arms in a single smooth motion, carrying her rapidly up the long path to the cabin. He didn't even let her go as he opened the door and strode across the living room into the cool haven of his bedroom. She clasped her arms around his neck and buried her head against his shoulder, pressing her wet hair into his cheek, weak with wanting him, with the racking, pulsating desire that only he could send pounding through her.

He set her down gently, and began to peel away the last barrier between them, the rough denim and smooth cotton that had already begun to dry in spots from the intensity of the summer sun. She stepped out of her sandals and felt the satiny oak floor under her feet, but that was all she really knew about her surroundings.

She was hardly conscious of where she was; her head was whirling with Jarod, only Jarod. She luxuriated in his masculine touch, in the dizzying feel and smell of him. She stood with her eyes closed while he removed the last of her damp clothing and brought the searing touch of his fingers to her skin.

Then his hands were gone. She murmured a protest; she opened her eyes. He was standing a little away from her, unbuttoning his own shirt, his eye roving appreciatively over her nakedness.

The shirt dropped away from his muscle-knotted shoulders and she took a step forward to put her hands on him, palms splayed in the middle of his smooth, copper-colored chest. She ran them over it, absorbing his contours through the pores of her skin, following the long hard muscles up to the heavy shoulders that seemed even wider now that they were uncovered.

His clothes forgotten, his fingertips came back to her shoulders to trace her tantalizing arms and then her sides and back, drawn to the silk of her skin by her seductive caress.

Then she reached for the silver oval of his buckle, slipping its hook from its place in the belt, and her lips touched his chest once, lightly, and then again. "Jarod," she whispered, "Jarod..."

The urgent need in him flamed into fire and he kicked out of his jeans and briefs with hard, sudden movements. He took her back into his arms and paced across the big room to the quilt-covered bed. "I've thought about this," he told her huskily as he laid her down. "I've lived this in my mind a million times while I was on the road—you and me together, here in my bed."

He stood for the space of a breath before he touched her again, one knee denting the mattress beside her. "You're one beautiful lady, Sabrina Dante, and I've wanted you since the minute I saw you."

She looked back at him without saying a word, completely unself-conscious in her happiness, glorying in his delight in her body and in his marvelous masculine perfection.

He then stretched out beside her, reaching a possessive arm to pull her to him, and slipped one of his long thighs between her own.

The rough palm of his hand began brushing the taut bud of her breast with a tingling friction that whorled out in ever widening circles of delight. His burning eyes held hers possessively. "I thought you wanted me in that first minute, too," he said, his hand moving to the other breast and giving it equal attention while his smoldering eyes beguiled hers. "Sabrina, do you want me?"

She caught her breath with the incredibility of his question as much as with the spearing pleasure of his touch. He *must* know that she wanted him. How could he possibly not when this shattering desire had been destroying her ability to think ever since the night they met?

"I want you, Jarod," she breathed and took into her hand the hard evidence of his need that was burning against her. "That's the one thing that I know for sure. I want you."

His eyes melted in response and he bent to replace his fingers with his lips, closing them around her nipple, pulling it into the sweet range of his tongue. The hot tension that it created there began to pound through her, escalating the need inside her until she thought she could not bear it.

Her hold on him tightened, then loosened again to caress him, and he pulled his mouth away from her breast to rain savage, ravening kisses over her face and hair, into the hollows of her collarbone, onto her throat and back onto her breasts again. She moaned with the need his lips set singing in her blood, and she arched against him, desperate for more ways to show him how she felt.

There were words echoing through her brain in rhythm with his kisses, I need you, Jarod, I need you so. But his lips came back to hers and kept her mute, so her hand left his throbbing masculinity to roam over his flat stomach, his back, his shoulders, to pull him up and over her.

Then he was above her, coming into her with a fierce primitive hunger, and those words and every other conscious thought disappeared, destroyed by the beginnings of a universe made only of flesh and feeling. His body was a part of hers now, the last distance between them was gone, and the jubilant fulfillment of this transported her completely.

They moved faultlessly together in the ageless rhythm that made them one, and stoked the fire that had brought them together into a conflagration that flamed higher and higher. Sabrina gave herself to the feeling with all her heart and soul. She let it seduce every part of her into a search for an end to this delightful torment.

Jarod took control of their movements. He slowed them, deliberately building the heat until it threatened to engulf them forever. She arched up to him and dug her fingers into the rock-hard muscles of his shoulders as the heat culminated at last in a shattering explosion that made her cry out his name with the last of her strength. She collapsed beneath him, trembling, and subsided into a golden rush of molten satisfaction.

He remained poised above her, in her, for an endless, sweet minute, then he rolled over on his side, pulling her with him to tuck her head into the warm hollow of his neck.

They lay completely sated, not speaking, all their need for words reduced to ashes in the blazing fire that had melted the two of them into one.

Chapter Seven

When Sabrina awoke it was to a long sultry twilight, quiet except for the buzzing litany of millions of locusts outside the open windows and the soft sounds of Jarod's breathing beside her. She nestled infinitesimally closer to him, even though her body was already curved into his, and began to softly stroke the sweat-dampened skin of his chest.

The movement almost aroused him and he moved away, then turned over, sprawling majestically across the bed like a sleeping lion. One of his arms came to rest on her abdomen, and even in his sleep it tightened proprietarily around her.

She smiled and hugged it to her, luxuriating in the wonder of being with him like this. It seemed like the most natural thing in the world, she marveled, glancing around the room that had seemed so alien to her only a few days before. Nothing else she'd done had ever seemed so natural or right.

Sabrina caressed the muscles of his forearm, hard and sinewy even in relaxation, then followed them up to the hard curve of his shoulder. She traced its shape, her fingertips loving each nuance of its contours. Then they moved into a little depression and stopped, feeling the bumpy ridge of scar tissue. It was shallow but long, running from his armpit almost to his collarbone.

He stirred and raised his hands to hers, tangling their fingers together. "Sabrina."

The word was a loving caress in the darkening room.

"Yes?"

He answered by moving her fingertips from his shoulder to his lips. He kissed each of them lightly, one at a time. "Hi," he whispered.

"Hello, Jarod." She loved the feel of his name on her lips..

Her hand moved over the hard, square line of his jaw and down his neck, back to the scar.

"Where did you get this?"

"Dogging," he answered lazily. "Had a wide jump. Came off too late and got hooked."

She thought about it for a minute. "I think you're going to have to translate that," she said. "I heard you but I don't know what you said."

He chuckled. "Steer wrestling. The steer was too far away from my horse and my timing was off. I landed on his horns with my shoulder instead of my hands."

She shivered as the picture formed in her mind. And his matter-of-fact tone made it even worse. He was talking about jumping off speeding horses and having his body ripped open by an animal's horns as casually as she might talk about ordering some new designs or having the display windows redone. *This* was what he did for a living. His life was in danger almost every day.

She tightened her arms around him.

"I can't stand to think about that," she said. "Jarod, it's too dangerous."

He shrugged. "You can walk across the street and get hit by a truck."

"You can but you don't have to go asking for it."

"I wasn't asking to get hooked!"

She laughed, but she buried her face in the hollow of his shoulder and covered the scar with it. "You know what I mean." *I wish you wouldn't ride in rodeos is what I mean.*

She thought about that. Where was the determination she'd had last night and this morning? Hadn't she decided to get off that emotional roller coaster and make this all business? How had she changed in these past few hours, especially the ones in his arms?

She didn't want to know the answer to that. Even the question scared her. She stirred and opened her eyes. "It's getting dark," she murmured.

He was stroking her hair. "I know. Do you need to call your mother?"

She flashed a questioning look at him, thinking that he was being silly.

"I'm serious. Last time we were here you called to report in."

"Too late," she said, chuckling dryly at the memory of Martin and her arrival home. "My brother gave me a hard time for not calling sooner."

His hand went still. "The brother we saw at Chi-Chi's?"

His tone was hard. Darn. What was it about Martin that made him so resentful? It was as bad as Martin's attitude toward him.

"Yes, I only have one brother." She tried to get off the subject. "About my mother—she's out of town. Nobody's waiting up for me tonight."

"Great. Then in that case I have some plans for you...."

His hand was moving again, over her back in seductively widening circles.

She laughed and pretended to pull away. "You mean we aren't getting back to the store before it closes?"

"We are not. I have plans for tonight that don't include the store in any way."

"So you *are* running out on your responsibilities!" She pulled back so she could see his eyes as she gave him a flirtatious smile. "What was that story about coming by here to check on the horses?"

"Later. We'll see them later." He rolled her over onto her back, holding her wrists as he bent to kiss her. "It's all a matter of priorities," he muttered against her lips. "As a businesswoman you know that. First things first, pretty lady."

His voice woke her from the other room. She opened her eyes to bright sunlight.

"Saturday night," he was saying into the telephone. "I'm on Daredevil. I oughtta be landing in Houston around five...."

She closed her eyes again, wishing she could close her ears as well. Saturday night.

She tried to think. Today was Thursday. Two days and he'd be gone.

He couldn't go; she'd just found what she'd always wanted in his arms. And he might get hurt. Who or what was Daredevil? Did he...it...have horns?

Sudden panic rushed through her, an intuitive fear that temporarily blocked the sun's light. She had to talk him out of it; maybe she could persuade him not to go.

His voice went on talking to some unseen person and she got out of bed and wrapped the sheet around her. She was in the doorway before she thought again. She looked at his face. It was absorbed in complete concentration on the arrangements he was making.

She had no right to try to talk him out of anything...why was she thinking this way? Had it actually happened just as she'd feared she would—had she fallen in love with him when they made love?

The thought made her suddenly weak and she leaned against the door for support.

He turned toward her as he hung up the phone.

She was completely irresistible, he thought. That answered the question he'd been asking himself all morning. Yesterday had ended the way it had because during that one day she'd been a fascinating contradiction of efficient businesswoman, intuitive bargainer with Molly Bear, surprisingly mischievous hoyden and fun-loving companion.

She'd also been a lonely little girl who needed him. That hidden vulnerability he'd sensed from the start made him want to protect Sabrina from the world.

In addition to all that, she was beautiful. Unconsciously he moved toward her. Her black hair tousled, her wide gray-blue eyes still misty with sleep, her white shoulder exposed by the drape of the sheet sent desire surging through him all over again.

"Good morning, sleepyhead."

His voice made her tremble with wanting.

She wrapped the sheet more tightly around her. She had to try to get some kind of control; she needed to think. When he touched her she *couldn't* think.

"Good morning."

She gave him a bright smile but retreated a step.

"You're already dressed," she said. "I'd better dress, too, so we can get on the road."

To Tulsa. To the store. She had to keep thinking about the store and what she needed to do there.

She turned back into the room, vaguely looking for her clothes. What was on her calendar for today?

"I have to give that last group of interviews," she told him. She gasped a little on the last word as his hand cupped her shoulder. She couldn't pull away; his skin was too sweet against hers.

"You have to see Angie, too," he said. "Remember?"

"I know, but..."

"I called Darlene earlier and she wants us to come over this afternoon and stay for supper. The whole family's getting together."

"Oh, we can't be here that long! We don't have time. We've got a store to open, remember?"

He trailed a shivery path of sensation up her neck with one fingertip. "We don't have much time for each other, either. I leave again Saturday and I could be gone as long as a month this time."

She sighed. "Oh, Jarod, I know. I heard you on the phone just now. I can't believe you're going again so soon."

She tried to think about the store, but his finger was tracing little circles under her ear.

"We're more important than the store. And there's Dorothy and Lawrence and a whole bunch of people who can handle whatever you're supposed to be doing."

Fear coursed through her again and with it resentment. He had no idea what she was supposed to be doing at the store—and no inkling of how hard she'd been working these past two weeks to make it what he wanted. How could he treat her work so lightly?

She jerked away. "Let me get dressed and we'll run by and see Angie," she said hotly. "It may seem incredible to you, but there are things that need doing at Jarod Redfeather that only I can do."

He caught her shoulders and spun her around to face him. "It may seem incredible to *you*, but there are things that need doing *with* Jarod Redfeather that only you can do," he growled.

She stared up at him. His dark eyes blazed down into hers; his hard fingers bit into her flesh. "I'm *not* taking you back to Tulsa today. That store's not going to be shot all to hell if you don't show up for a couple of days."

"You'll take me back if I want to go!"

The intensity in his eyes lightened with the old mischief and that ingenuous grin curved his sensual lips.

"But do you?" he asked, very softly. "Do you want to go back?"

She tried to hold on to her anger, but it was a losing battle. She felt the corners of her mouth begin to lift.

He saw it, too.

"I want you, Sabrina. I want you so damn much. And in these two days I have to get enough of loving you to last me a whole month of long, cold nights."

The words went to the very heart of her. She lifted her face to his. Their mouths met.

He took her hands away from the sheet and together they let it slide to the floor.

The whole day was like a dream. They finally got out of bed long enough to cook omelets and to wander down to the pasture to see the horses, but they were never apart for more than a few minutes. Sabrina didn't let herself think at all; that same sense of unreasoning joy that had captured them the day before held them in an impenetrable cocoon. There was no other reality.

In the middle of the afternoon they went in to Tahlequah to buy something new for Sabrina to wear to Darlene's, but they saw no one that they knew. Modeling sundresses for Jarod's approval in the quaint little dress shop in town was just another adventure in their own fantasy land. By the time they were dressed and on their way to Darlene's, Sabrina felt that she and Jarod were the only people in the whole world.

That sensation was destroyed the minute they got out of the truck. They were greeted with shrieks of "J-a-r-o-d!" in high childish voices, and it seemed to Sabrina that a dozen children of all sizes and ages abandoned their outdoor games and ran to surround them.

The youngest, a chubby toddler called Jesse, held up his arms to Jarod and demanded to be held. Another, slightly older, wanted his turn, too, and Jarod complied, settling one onto each shoulder.

"Mama and Aunt Darlene and Granny are cooking," a little girl piped. "They're making fry bread."

"And connuche, too," another added.

Their big black eyes examined Sabrina shyly, but neither of them was bold enough to speak to her. They melted into the group swirling around Jarod's long legs for the walk up to the house, and by the time they reached the yard Sabrina was trailing behind.

They went in through the back door that opened directly into Darlene's modest kitchen. The women-folk greeted them with a chorus of delighted squeals and a flurry of hugs for Jarod. In all the confusion it was hard for Sabrina to catch everyone's name; the house seemed to be packed with people, and every time another group discovered Jarod's presence there was a new wave of voices to drown out the introductions.

In what seemed to be only a matter of seconds, Jarod had been swallowed up into a crowd of men that was filling the living room and spilling over onto the front and out into the yard. The children were every-where, in and out of the house, but the adults appeared to be segregated by sex and Sabrina was left in the kitchen with the other women.

One of them, who was about Sabrina's age, indicated a chair at the table. "Would you like to sit here?" she asked with a shy smile. "You can just watch us; we won't make you work on your very first visit."

"I'd be glad to help if someone would show me what to do."

A chorus of quiet demurrals answered her and she sat down, wishing fervently that she had something to do with her hands.

Across the table from her a wizened little woman was pounding up hickory nuts and forming the result-ing powder into balls. "Could I help you?" Sabrina asked. "What are you making?"

"Soup. Connuche."

She went on with her work without another word and after a minute or so Sabrina decided that the answer to her first question must be "no." She watched the old woman's gnarled fingers as they worked, wondering if there was any way she could get out of the room and go find Jarod. He'd been beside her so constantly for these past hours . . . no, days, he'd been her world. She was lost without him.

She glanced around the room. A tall matronly woman was standing at the stove dropping triangles of fry bread dough into sizzling deep fat, the girl who offered her the chair was taking pies from the oven, some others were washing dishes at the sink. They were all chattering and laughing, but none of them had time to entertain a visitor.

She took a hickory nut from the bowlful in front of her and reached for the nutcracker. She fitted the nut into place and squeezed it hard. It fell in pieces out into the plastic tablecloth and she picked through it absently. Well, so much for fantasy land, she thought. Here's reality.

A little chill ran through her. This was home to Jarod, this whole scene that was so strange to her. He, no doubt, was having a wonderful time.

A picture of him in her mother's house flashed across her mind. What was it he had said? This is a little different from most of the places down in the hills where I come from.

And then she remembered the fit he'd thrown about her remodeling her new home.

She took a sharp pick from the wooden bowl and jabbed at the nutmeat. Those differences couldn't be *too* important, she thought, they just couldn't. Not after everything they'd just shared. There was not way Martin's fears could prove to be valid, after all. Was there?

She looked up to see Angie coming through the screened back door.

"I just saw Jarod and he told me you were here," she said. She stopped to stand shyly beside the table. "We're glad you could come."

Sabrina stood, too, grateful for an excuse to escape. "Thank you, Angie. It's good to see you."

She meant it; she truly liked the girl. "You're one of the reasons I'm here," she said. "When we go back to Tulsa tonight I want to take your paintings to the store."

Angie dropped her eyes. "I have some picked out for you," she said.

"Aren't you excited about our selling your work?" Sabrina asked enthusiastically. "I'm so glad Jarod thought of it. It's very good and I want lots of people to see it."

"Thank you."

"Let's go see which ones you've chosen for me..." Sabrina began. The woman at the stove, whom she thought Jarod had introduced as his sister, Darlene, interrupted.

"Angie, let's get the tea on the table. We're ready to feed the men and the kids," she called.

The women began carrying glasses of iced tea and steaming platters and bowls of food into the small dining room where the men were gathering. They also set places for the children in the kitchen. Sabrina tried to help, but she kept getting in the way, and by the time everyone was seated she was ready to scream with frustration.

Jarod ruffled her hair possessively as he passed her on the way to his place at the table and they exchanged smiles, but there was no chance to talk; he was deep into a conversation about horses with two of the other men. She watched him from the kitchen doorway, feeling lonely and bereft. He wasn't hers anymore. All of these people had taken him away.

She moved nervously around the kitchen while the men and children ate and the women waited on the two tables. She watched the children and smiled at their antics in spite of her uncomfortableness. When Angie came to stand beside her she entertained herself by trying to learn all of their names.

At last the men finished and went outside; Darlene and Angie cleared that table and set it again. The women gathered around it and Darlene had Sabrina sit between her and Angie. They explained the preparation of the traditional Cherokee dishes to her. Everyone tried to include her in the general conversation, but all of them were shy and reserved, and the talk kept turning to family and tribal activities that Sabrina knew nothing about.

Sabrina made a few more remarks to Angie about the paintings and they talked a little about the arts and crafts department of the store. Soon, however, one of the cousins across the table started telling a long story about a contest to be held during the Cherokee national holiday and Sabrina was left to her own devices again.

She played with the strange-tasting food, remembering Jarod's remark when he'd given her the fry bread at the powwow. She *still* wasn't ready for connuche, she thought, with a little secret smile.

She took a tiny bite and then stared into space, her discomfort growing. If only she didn't feel so out of place, she thought. She and the others had tried, but somehow she was still out of place in this heritage she wanted so badly to share.

Because Jarod wasn't beside her.

A little shock ran through her with the thought. She wanted him to be with her. Every minute. She wanted him to be there when she tasted the connuche; she wanted him to be there to explain the people and the happenings in the stories she was hearing. She wanted that sense of utter rightness that came to her only when she was with him.

Frustration began to build along with her discomfort. What was that line Jarod had used that morning when she wanted to go back to the store? We don't have much time for each other, he'd said. Well, this wasn't time with each other, and if she wasn't going to be with him she needed to be at work. It would be a veritable miracle if they opened on time, and her being away for two days certainly hadn't helped things any.

She glanced at her watch. If they were going to arrive in Tulsa so she could talk with Dorothy before closing time, they needed to leave within the hour.

She tried to hide her impatience until Angie had finished her dessert.

"Angie, I don't want to rush you, but could we see the paintings now and get them wrapped for traveling?" She smiled apologetically at Darlene. "I'm sorry, but I really need to get back to the store before closing time if I can."

"That's all right."

She and Angie excused themselves and went to Angie's room, which she obviously shared with a younger child. An easel was set up in front of the window, on the opposite side of the room from a bed surrounded by toys. It held a large canvas that was about half finished, and some shelves in the corner nearby held more in varying stages of completion.

"I like this one," Sabrina said, standing in front of the easel while Angie went to open the closet. "Maybe you'll let me have it when you're finished."

"Maybe," Angie said. "It's the legend of the first fire."

She took three paintings from the closet and went over to spread them on the bed. Two were medium-size oils, the other was a miniature. One of the larger ones was a landscape, the other two were historical scenes of Indian life.

"These are the ones I have ready for you now."

Sabrina looked them over carefully. "They're good," she pronounced. "I like them." She turned back to Angie. "But where's my favorite, *Triumphal Journey*? I thought I was supposed to get it, too."

Angie's eyes slid away from hers. "I . . . I need to keep it awhile."

"Oh?" Sabrina frowned at her, perplexed. "I thought we agreed on the phone the other day that you were going to sell it."

Angie busily began to wrap the paintings that were on the bed. "I need to work on it some more," she said. "I decided that it isn't finished."

She kept her head bent over the packages she was tying. Sabrina reached to hold the string for her.

"All right," she said. "How about if I pick it up when I come to get the first dress from Molly Bear?"

Angie gave her consent with a brief nod and they carried the packages out into the living room.

"Let's take these on out to the truck," Sabrina suggested. "Then I'll find Jarod and we'll say our goodbyes. We need to start back to Tulsa."

"I think he's right outside," Angie said, holding the front door open for her.

Jarod was under the shade of the enormous hackberry tree that dominated the yard, sitting easily on his haunches. Ridge was near him in a ladder-backed chair, leaning against the tree trunk. Several other men were sitting or standing around them. They were all absorbed in their conversation and none of them looked up at the sound of the door.

"See? There he is with Daddy and Grandpa Ridge."

"Yes."

On their way to the truck they passed within a few yards of the group, and Sabrina looked at Jarod, hoping to signal him that she was ready to leave. But his face was turned away from her.

The late sunlight dappled his hair and skin through the leaves; in his short-sleeved brown shirt he looked as if he were a part of the tree's broad trunk. And he looked just that immovable. He didn't even know she was there.

Chapter Eight

Jarod watched Sabrina walk down to the truck. He liked the way she held herself, the way she moved. He'd noticed it the first time he saw her—when she'd turned and looked at him in that cool, composed way. It was a look that he'd thought haughty until he'd seen that . . . searching under it. And noticed the fire deep in her eyes.

"Beautiful woman, all right," his brother-in-law, Billy Fourkiller, said. He nodded conversationally as if agreeing with something Jarod had said out loud.

Jarod's eyes flicked to him.

Billy fingered a flat can of chewing tobacco out of his shirt pocket and took a pinch before he spoke again. "Uh-huh, she's really somethin'. Remember seein' her once when I was workin' for Dante Oil." He fitted the tobacco into his cheek and put the lid back onto the can. "Surprises me she's your latest choice, though." He glanced sideways at Jarod with a sudden, sharp concern. "Figured you'd had enough of that high-class society type to last you the rest of your life."

Jarod's answer was a noncommittal grunt, but he felt his nerves tighten. He didn't want to think about the past, nor about the differences between him and Sabrina. There certainly hadn't been any differences yesterday afternoon and last night.

He glanced away from Billy, looking for her. She and Angie were halfway back up the hill. They weren't talking much, he noticed.

Instead of returning to the house as he expected, Sabrina stopped in front of him.

"Jarod, I hate to interrupt, but don't you think we should be starting back? I'd planned to drop in at the store before closing time."

Irritation washed over him. What was she doing worrying about the store at a time like this? This was supposed to be a sociable evening. He probably wouldn't get to see everybody again for a month.

He stood, stretching slowly up to his full height, then leaned back against the big tree. "Had you?" he drawled.

Billy said, "Might just as well stay over. No sense in runnin' back up to Tulsa tonight and right back down here tomorrow."

Sabrina stopped trying to read Jarod's expression and looked at Billy instead. "What do you mean come back tomorrow?"

He stood up, then, too, his black eyes twinkling. "Jarod's promised to let us show him up at the rodeo tomorrow night," he said. "Be a whole lot tougher competition than he thinks."

Jarod grinned. "It would be funny if you guys beat my scores."

"Come out early and we'll let you get in some practice; you're gonna need all the help you can get," Billy continued to tease. "Can't stay in Tulsa till the last minute and expect to do any good."

"I'm not going back to Tulsa until I show you up for the braggart you are," Jarod drawled.

What was he talking about? Anger flared through Sabrina; she fought to keep it out of her voice.

"Well, *you* may not have to get back to work," she said firmly, giving him a direct look. "But I do. I've already missed two whole days...."

He stared back at her, angry now. It wasn't her place to decide when they'd leave. She sounded as if she was trying to tell him what to do. Right in front of his whole family.

He straightened up and moved toward her. "*I'll* decide when you have to go back to work," he said, putting a steely hand on her arm. "Right now we're working on that education I promised you. It's about time you saw a rodeo; any red-blooded Oklahoman who's one-sixteenth Cherokee ought to go to at least one."

"But I..."

His fingers tightened. "We'd better go tell Darlene and the girls goodbye now so you can get all rested up for the big event."

"Yeah, sometimes it's way into the wee hours of the mornin' before the show's over," Billy put in.

They walked up to the house in stony silence and made their goodbyes. On the way out again Jarod kept her waiting as he stopped to exchange a few last remarks about the rodeo with Billy and Ridge. When finally they were alone in the pickup she was shaking with anger.

"I cannot *believe* this!" she stormed. "I've been expecting us to go back to Tulsa tonight. We have to. We'll never get the store open if we stay down here all the time!"

His eyes raked hers with a brief stony glance, then he stared into the rearview mirror as he backed the truck, very fast, down the drive and into the road. He straightened it out and savagely shifted gears. "I didn't get up and walk out in the middle of a visit so we could talk about the damned store." His tone was quiet, a startling contrast to her tempestuous one, but every word was bitingly clear.

"We'd better be discussing the store," she shot back. "That's the most important thing we could possibly be talking about—how to set it up so it'll make money."

His glance flicked to her, then back to the road. "Making money," he repeated thoughtfully. "The most important thing in the world, huh?"

His very stillness suddenly communicated his feelings to her. He was as angry as she.

"Right!" she said passionately. "You may not have noticed it, Jarod, but making a profit *is* actually the reason that people start a business in the first place."

"I've noticed."

The heavy sarcasm in his voice fueled her anger. "Well, if that's the way you feel, why did you get into this, anyway?" She rushed on without giving him time to answer. "Whatever your reasons are, *mine* are to make the store successful. It has to be a success. I'm investing my whole career in it."

"I'm investing several years of blood and broken bones in it, myself," he said angrily. "But I don't intend to let it take over my whole life."

"No problem there," she shot back. "So far it doesn't seem to have taken more than five minutes of your time."

His eyes flashed to hers, piercingly bright in the gathering dusk.

"Some things are more important than success," he bit out fiercely. "Much more. I need to be with my family and friends."

"You've just been with them, for heaven's sake!" she exploded. "And there's no reason for us to hang around for a whole day waiting to see them again at that rodeo." She glared at his stony profile. "After all, Jarod, you don't have to *move* down here!"

"Yes, I do," he replied in that flat, closed tone that she hated. "This is where I belong."

"Well, I don't!"

"That's easy enough to see. You've been taught all your life that financial success is the end goal of everything and you need to be where you can put that into practice. You're living up to that philosophy very well."

"I am not!"

"You are. You ruined a good time back there. And for what?"

"To try to get *your* store open." She was practically choking, she was so angry. "I was just trying to do my job, Jarod, not to prove that money is all important. I had no idea when we left the store that I wouldn't be back for a week."

"Well, you can stay away one more day. Tomorrow I want to have a good time with my friends."

"And tonight I want to go back to Tulsa. If you won't drive me, then take me to the bus station."

He didn't reply.

"Tahlequah does have a bus station, doesn't it? Or a taxi. I'll take a taxi."

They had almost reached the entrance to his private road.

"Jarod! Turn around!"

He slowed the truck and punched the button that opened the gate.

"Take me to town this instant!" she demanded, her voice shaking with fury.

He drove through the gate, closed it and stomped on the accelerator. "I'd like nothing better," he said in a vicious drawl. "But I couldn't live with knowing I left you sitting out on the street on a bench all night."

"There are no buses tonight?"

"Bus would be more like it. I think maybe there's one a day or something like that."

She seethed in silence until he parked the truck in a turnaround. The minute it stopped moving she leaped out and as soon as he unlocked the cabin's door she was inside. She flicked on the light and went straight to the telephone in the kitchen.

"Where's your directory?"

"In the drawer."

She picked up the receiver in one hand and jerked open the drawer with the other. She used more force than she had intended, and it came completely out of the cabinet. The telephone directory, plus what seemed to be dozens of pieces of paper—business cards, names and numbers on envelopes and napkins, and rodeo schedules—fell out, fluttering all over the floor in the breeze from the open door.

"Oh, no!" she breathed.

Jarod crossed the room to take the heavy drawer from her hand. His fingers brushed hers, and even in her anger she felt a thrill run through her.

She tried to push his hand away, dropping to her knees to begin picking up the papers while he put the drawer away.

A slow, strong, older woman's voice flowed out of the dangling receiver. "Why, honey, she must've been married four or five times at the very least," she was saying.

Startled, Sabrina glanced at the phone, then at Jarod, who had dropped down to help her. "Party line," he said, reaching for the receiver to replace it.

Before he could complete the motion, the calm voice continued. "Matter of fact, I told her once, right to her face, I says, 'Mattie Lou, looks to me like you don't care *who* the man is, just so's he's breath and britches.'"

Sabrina stared at the receiver in astonishment. Then she looked at Jarod and saw her surprise and amusement mirrored in his face.

They burst into laughter, kneeling there in the middle of the kitchen floor, looking into each other's eyes with quick delight. Their anger fragmented in it and then dissolved; they couldn't stop laughing until tears were running down their cheeks.

He reached out to brush hers away. "...who's that?" the voice on the phone demanded. "I said..."

Without looking at the instrument he replaced it in its cradle. His eyes were fast on Sabrina's.

The room was silent except for their breathing and the rustling of the papers.

"We don't need to answer any questions," he murmured, tilting her face up to his. "We don't have time for such nonsense as that."

"And neither does Mattie Lou," she said with an impish smile.

"I don't know how I'm going to break this to you," he said slowly, his lips very close to hers. "But I really don't give a damn about Mattie Lou's love life. I just want to think about mine."

Their lips touched. Desire, pure and hot, sprang to life in her loins and her whole body went weak with it.

He cupped her head in both his hands and held it still, settling his lips onto hers like a bee settling onto a flower. His tongue explored their petals, then plunged into the deep secret of her mouth, determined to drink every drop of sweet nectar that it held.

Blindly she reached out to steady herself. Her hands first found his arms, then the rock-hard muscles of his shoulders and clung to them as if she were drowning.

She twined her tongue with his.

He groaned and brought his mouth down on hers with an even more bruising power, kissing her with a vehement passion that took her breath away. She held him to her and let him obliterate the world.

At last he began getting to his feet, pulling her with him, not letting a modicum of space come between them. He tore his lips from her mouth and burned a wandering trail over the curve of her throat as he picked her up in his arms.

"I want you," he muttered hoarsely. "Let's go to bed."

But they made it only as far as the couch in the living room because she couldn't keep her hands out of his hair or her lips away from the hollow of his throat. They sank into the deep cushions, clinging together as if they were going into danger.

His lips feathered over her hair, his breathing was deep and ragged in her ear. He was untying the straps of her dress that crossed on her back, and every touch of his fingertips against her bare skin sent a charge of electricity through her veins.

She breathed his name without even being aware that she had spoken. She slipped her hands into his shirt, then ran them over the rugged contours of his chest with increasing urgency, pulling the snap fasteners apart one after the other. When the shirt was pushed back to the tops of his shoulders she circled her palms on his skin, moving them gradually outward to tease the hard, flat nipples.

His hands went still on her back and he leaned a little away from her, not moving at all. He let her tantalize him for an endless minute, then he reached for her.

"You've been to a shaman," he muttered hoarsely. "You've learned a charm to use on me."

She laughed, deep in her throat.

He bent her back across his arm. Her lips parted under his, tempting him, inviting him. He went willingly into their sweet trap, thrusting his tongue deep, ever deeper into the secret warmth.

She gave herself to him and took him into her at the same time, reaching up to run her fingers hungrily into the thick silk of his hair. She tried to pull him closer.

He wouldn't let her; he held her a little bit away and his mouth left hers to kiss her ear and then to move purposefully down the sensitive side of her neck. The kisses trailed over her naked skin to the hollow between her breasts, not even hesitating as he reached the thin cotton of her dress.

She cradled his head in her hands delicately, carefully. The anticipation made her breath tighten in her throat. His mouth moved slowly over the swelling curve of her breast and stopped, hot and moist, to enclose its hard, taut bud.

He tugged at it for a moment, sending golden shafts of pleasure through her veins.

Then that heat was gone and he was loosening her straps again, using both hands to pull the flimsy fabric of the dress away. He let it drop to her waist and took her breasts into his hands.

She contracted with exquisite sensation, watching his face in the spill of early moonlight through the windowed wall. She loved his intense absolute absorption in her and her alone. He was searching her face, looking for her soul, it seemed. Then his eyes moved away from hers to follow his hands.

"I can't get enough of you," he murmured, his voice raspy with desire. "I want you every time I look at you."

Then, with a shuddering sigh he bent to add his mouth to the sweet torment at her breasts. His lips, his teeth and tongue nipped and drew on one of them, then the other, and she tangled her fingers into his hair to hold them there, to impel him not to stop, not ever.

Not until he wrung the cry from her, "Love me. Jarod, I need you to love me."

He let her go and bent to tug at one boot and then the other, kicking them off while he undid his belt buckle. His skin was glowing like burnished copper in the subdued light and there was no way she could keep her hands off it. She reached to stroke the symmetrical muscles of his broad back with her palms as she had done to his chest, spreading her fingers out so that she could absorb his masculine beauty through each of her pores, so she could soak it up to feed the hunger that had been raging in her all evening.

Then she was on her knees behind him on the wide sofa, her arms under his. Her hands slid over his chest, then down his rib cage on each side to slip under the waistband of his jeans as he began to undo the metal buttons, and finally under his narrow cotton briefs to find a driving masculinity that made her go weak all over. His hands stopped moving and he turned his wind-roughened face into the curve of her shoulder.

"Oh, Sabrina," he said on the strength of one ragged breath. "Sabrina, your hands..."

He rubbed his cheek against her satiny skin and then, with an effort, drew more air into his lungs. "Sabrina, love, you are one sexy lady."

He shrugged out of the clothes and let them fall, then turned to face her. "Stay right there," he murmured as he took her arms into his strong hands to help her balance in the downy cushions. "Don't you move." Slowly, delectably, he went to his knees on the floor and began to place careful kisses on the first snowy swell of each breast and then on the tips, giving the caresses at random, but imbuing every one with the urgent message of his need.

His mouth moved lower, and as it reached the obstruction of her clothes again, he pushed the dress down over her slim hips, only to reveal a lacy half slip.

"All this keeps getting in my way," he told her very seriously. "We're going to have to get rid of it."

She cupped his head in her hand, then trailed one finger up the side of his neck and around and into his ear. "I'll help if you will," she murmured huskily.

They laughed conspiratorially as they began to remove the offending bits of cotton, lace and silk, but their movements grew progressively more clumsy and slow when she lay back on the couch and as his lips followed after hers and they started to exchange intense, yearning kisses. At last her legs were free and naked to his touch and he explored their sleek length with slow, seductive hands that made her pulse stand still.

"That's better," he muttered huskily. "You're most beautiful of all just like this."

He continued the unhurried strokes up onto the trembling flesh of her abdomen and then, with a fierceness that made her gasp and knot her fingers into his hair, he replaced his hands with his lips. Suddenly he was holding her in an iron grip, his fingertips digging deep into the tender flesh of her hips while he rained searching, savage kisses onto her naked body.

His lips left a burning brand every place they touched, a mark that she thought through her haze of passion would be there for the rest of her life. She would wear the visible sign that her body had been created for him and his for her.

Sabrina moaned with the agony of wanting that he was fanning to a fever pitch inside her. She tried to form his name with lips that were trembling and ravenous for the taste of his. Her hands left his hair to find his muscled shoulders, to urge him mutely to lie on the cushions beside her, to give her his mouth again and the whole glorious length of his hard body.

He murmured a wordless assent, but he lingered for an incredibly tantalizing moment over the throbbing tips of her breasts. His teeth and tongue, his relentless lips hovered there, teasing and caressing them until she thought they would burst with the insistence of the desire he was stimulating.

It wrested a beseeching whimper from her that brought him onto the deep cushions of the sofa, at first beside her, then over her, his long body fitting hers perfectly, his mouth melding itself into hers with an all-consuming passion.

He raised himself above her, just enough so that their skins could brush languidly against each other, could commune in a delicate, age-old touch that needed no words. She moved under him, with him, stroking against him as if she were afraid he'd break the contact. Finally when the full, warm ache inside her could wait no longer to be assuaged, she arched up to him.

They joined together then and the magic spun tighter as their movements fell into a cadence that had none of the flirtatious touching of the moment before. He drove into her and she twined her arms around his neck, then ran her hands down the long curve of his back to cup his small, muscular hips and urge him on.

They were a part of each other, they were one, and she held him to her, in her, with a wild, sumptuous joy for that miraculous truth. They climbed higher and higher into a fantasy union that fused them irrevocably, transported them into a shimmering dream of undulating movement, a vision of coppery light and ivory shadows in the creamy glow of the moonlight.

At the very last minute he tore his mouth from her and buried his face in the warm hollow of her neck, moaning her name in a voice husky and rough with his passion. "Sabrina..." he said, his breath hot against her skin, and then they fell over the edge of reality together into a waiting sensuous paradise that caught and held them suspended in its golden net.

Afterward they lay together with his head against her heart, his hand roaming languorously over her moist body, stopping here and there to reaffirm an old claim. She traced her fingers in and out of his sweat-dampened hair, trailing their tips along the side of his cheek, memorizing the bones of his rugged face.

At last he moved, stretching out against the back of the sofa and cradling her on one arm so that their faces would be only inches apart. He caressed her face with his shadowy dark eyes for a long, long moment. Then, his eyelids, heavy with sated passion, closed.

She lay in the curve of his long body, watching his face. Finally she lifted her hand and touched his cheek, then traced the deep curve of his brow with one fingertip, willing him to come awake and talk to her.

A wrenching longing was filling her, an urgent need to know what thoughts had been behind that last, dark gaze. Scenes and sensations, snatches of conversation and bits of remembered feelings from all the times they'd been together flashed through her mind, turning behind her eyes like colored slides on a wheel. She'd been with him for many hours now, she'd made love with him, but she had no idea how he really felt about her. Was this as important for him as it was for her?

She glanced down at the contrast of their skins—his red arm across the creamy white of her body—and then looked around the rustic room that was so definitely his. She closed her eyes and turned onto her side, her face away from his, but she edged her back more firmly into the spoon fit of their bodies.

She tightened her eyes closed and let the memory of their lovemaking wash over her. She had no idea what his feelings were for her, and there was no way at this moment that she could face what she was feeling for him.

Chapter Nine

Jarod stopped halfway up the rickety wooden bleachers and squinted back at the little dirt-floored arena. He led Sabrina into a row of seats.

"This should be a good spot; you'll be able to see all the action from here."

He sounded so casual and cheerful that it made her want to scream.

"Then I'd better move. I don't *want* to see all the action."

He chuckled. "Remember what I told you about getting hit crossing the street? We were in more danger driving here from my place than I will be in the arena."

"I doubt that!"

He smiled and shook his head, reaching out to touch her hair. He brushed a strand of it away from her face. "Sabrina, the fear is just part of the game. You get used to it."

"Maybe you do."

The smile metamorphosed into his crooked grin. "I even like it."

That was true, she thought. She'd felt his anticipation building since early afternoon.

She squinted up at him, every plane of his face lit by the late afternoon sun, and shaped the high bone of one cheek with her thumb.

"You'd just better not get hurt," she whispered fiercely.

"I won't."

He covered her hand with his and gently lowered it to her side. "You sit down here now and make yourself comfortable. Darlene and Angie will probably come along pretty soon; they'll keep you company."

He touched her hair again, a quick, light caress that was gone too soon, and left. She watched him until he disappeared behind the chutes. He didn't look back.

She sat down and glanced around at the crowd: at the children running up and down the swaying steps and the groups staking their claims by spreading blankets over the benches. She didn't see a single person she knew.

It was just as well, she thought. She really didn't want to try to make conversation with Darlene or Angie. The evening before had been bad enough.

Sharp loneliness pierced her again. He wasn't really hers at all. Making love with him, being with him for two days had made her feel that he was. But the rodeo could snatch him away as completely as his family had done last night. Then she'd be more alone than she could ever have imagined before she met him.

It was foolhardy and dangerous to be getting so involved with him, she lectured herself silently. She'd known, somehow, from the very beginning that if they ever made love...

"Hello."

Darlene was standing in the aisle beside her, the toddler, Jesse, balanced on one hip.

"Jarod said you were here."

"Hi, Darlene." Sabrina moved over. "Join me. I'm just sitting here dreading to see someone fall off a horse or get chased by a bull."

Darlene sat down beside her and settled Jesse on her lap.

Sabrina ruffled his hair. "Hi, Jesse."

He replied with a slow, sideways look and a faint smile.

"They don't usually get hurt too bad," Darlene said comfortingly. "Billy's been riding off and on for years and he hasn't been to the hospital but twice."

Sabrina shivered. "But Jarod was gored once...."

Darlene nodded and smoothed Jesse's black hair. "He's rode many a bull since then, though." She gave Sabrina a shy smile. "He'll be all right." That seemed to settle it as far as Darlene was concerned, and as the music from the small band blared, she turned to watch the first horses of the grand entry come into the arena.

Sabrina's eyes followed hers, but she was hardly aware of the galloping horses and colorful flags. Jarod had told her the bull riding was the last event. She had to sit here for two or three hours before she knew whether he'd be all right.

She glanced toward the chutes, but he was nowhere in sight. She should have gone back to Tulsa last night. Even if she'd had to walk.

"Hey, Jarod! You seen Darlene?"

Billy's voice broke his concentration. He stopped the stretching exercises and straightened; Billy and his cousin, Ray Pigeon, were coming toward him. Billy was carrying a sack of popcorn; Ray held two beers. He offered one to Jarod as they came up to him.

Jarod shook his head. "I'm riding."

"I need to find Darlene," Billy repeated. "Forgot to give her any money. Jesse's probably already fussing to go to the concession stand."

"I sent her up there to sit with Sabrina," Jarod said, jerking his head toward the bleachers. "She needed some company."

"Sabrina! Is that her name?" Ray demanded. "That good-looking girl that come in with you? She the one needs company?"

Jarod nodded shortly and bent to look for his glove in his rigging bag. Ray sounded as if he was already about half drunk; he didn't want to discuss Sabrina with him.

"Well, I'll be glad to go sit with her," Ray went on. "When I seen you all drive up I thought she was one of the best-looking women been around here in a long time." He took a swig from the can of beer. "By the way," he persisted loudly. "What's her last name?"

"Dante," Billy supplied helpfully. "Remember when we used to work for Dante Oil? One of *those* Dantes."

"Whooee!" Ray whooped. He slapped Jarod on the shoulder as he straightened up. "You're in the big time now, ain't you, boy?"

"Don't worry about it," Jarod said shortly. He tried to ignore Ray and began working his glove.

"I cain't help but worry about it," Ray said. "Why, you're liable to git into trouble in a situation like that."

Jarod looked up and gave him a hard stare, but Ray didn't notice; he was tilting the can to his mouth again.

"Yessir," he said, lowering it and wiping his lips with the back of his hand, "you better let me help you. Us ol' country boys gotta stick together. Them bored society girls can be too much for just one of us to handle. They come around here lookin' for some new, ex-otic plaything to light up their life, we need to give 'em more than they bargained for...."

"Shut up, Ray," Jarod snapped. His eyes flashed to Billy. "Get him out of here."

Billy pulled at Ray's arm. "Come on. Go talk to the calf ropers while I take this money to Darlene." He managed to move Ray a few steps. "See you later, Jarod. Good luck."

"Yeah, good luck," Ray echoed. He looked at Jarod over his shoulder. "You're gonna need it, man. You're a little bit outta your class this time around."

Jarod didn't reply; he looked back down in his glove and tried to erase the sound of those words in his ears. But they wouldn't go away, they reverberated around and around inside his skull. Ray might be half drunk and green with jealousy, but he wasn't stupid.

He thought again of the way she'd looked when he left her, the sunlight gleaming against the impenetrable black of her hair. She'd looked the same, but she hadn't been her usual self. She'd been quieter, tenser, just as she had been at Darlene's the evening before.

He fitted the glove into every crevice of his hand and punched at it viciously with the other fist. Ray was right. Sabrina didn't belong here.

He dipped into the resin and worked it thoroughly into every inch of the leather. He was more than a little bit out of his class this time around—hell, he was out of his mind.

Sabrina watched the crowd and the calf roping while sipping at the cold soda Billy had bought her. Even in the sultry heat the liquid was hard to swallow. Fear had formed a lump in her throat that made it difficult for her even to breathe. Billy had gone and Darlene was sitting quietly beside her, rocking gently back and forth with Jesse asleep on her shoulder. She'd hardly talked for what seemed like hours, and Sabrina felt alien in the middle of the festive crowd as she had in the midst of the family at Darlene's house.

There was a thump, then a resounding clatter from the chutes. A gasp swept through the audience and Sabrina leaned forward, straining to see what was happening.

A pale-gray Brahma bull was kicking the sides of the chute, rattling the boards and making the posts sway in their moorings. Several cowboys were working to secure the back gate; the bull deliberately aimed a kick at one of them. Sabrina's breath caught in her throat as the man jumped out of the way. Her eyes searched the chute area for Jarod; surely this wasn't the bull that he would ride.

But it was. There he was, climbing the side of the chute, casually balancing himself with one hand, holding a leather strap in the other. Her heart stopped as he reached the top and balanced with one foot on either side of the wall, his leg only inches from the plunging, twisting head.

The animal's horns were sharp and curving. Its pallid, almost-white color gave it an aura of pure evil. Unconsciously, Sabrina twisted her fingers into the thin strap of her bag. She ought to get up and leave. She could go sit in the truck until this was over.

But she couldn't take her eyes away, not even when Jarod swung his leg over the top and dropped down into the chute. Somehow, miraculously, he seemed to be putting the rope around the bull's huge middle, then, abruptly, he was sitting on its back, directing, as two other cowboys pulled to tighten the rope. The bull was moving around erratically, banging Jarod's chaps against the sides of the chute, and she stood up to try to see his face.

It was hidden under the wide brim of his hat. His head was tucked down and he seemed to be completely absorbed in rubbing the rope through his gloved hand. Her eyes were glued to him, but he didn't look up. There was no connection between them now; it was like the night before when he'd forgotten that she existed.

He seemed to be trapped forever in the chute, on top of that uncontrollable mass of lethal muscle and bone. Then the announcer called out his name and he grasped the hand-hold on the rope, wrapped it around once and appeared to sink down deeper into the loose hide of the bull's back. He raised his left hand high and nodded once, abruptly. The gate flew open and they were outside, whirling toward her.

The bull's front feet hit the ground directly in front of the stands, close enough so that Sabrina could hear his angry snorts. She bit her lip. If Jarod should fall off now . . .

But he stuck to the animal's back, his powerful body adapting itself to the jarring rhythm and quick movements. She could see his face now, but it told her nothing; he was captured by a concentration on something far away.

One of his arms curved above his head for balance and, in spite of her fear, the beauty of the scene caught her. His perfect physique and strong profile were outlined for a second in the lights against the black sky and she felt a shimmering shaft of hot desire.

Then the bull backed away from her and the eight seconds of the ride became the most interminable ones of her life. After an aeon had passed, the raucous whistle blew and Jarod reached to unfasten the last wrap of the rope around his hand. He waited for another second, for just the right moment, and then he jumped, pushing against the bull's back to force himself as far away from it as possible.

He landed in a sitting position and before he could get to his feet the bull turned to look for him. Instinctively, Sabrina screamed warning, praying that the rodeo clown would be fast enough to come between them.

He wasn't, but he rolled his barrel in front of the questing horns and then rushed in close to them himself, his baggy pants flopping in the breeze, waving a flag in the bull's face.

Jarod got up, dusted off the seat of his pants, then calmly collected his hat and his rigging. He began walking back toward the chutes. His only indication that he wasn't completely alone in the world was one upraised hand acknowledging the cheers and shouts of the crowd.

The audience was roaring, but Sabrina was quiet, hardly aware of the noise or of the equally silent Darlene beside her. How could he do this?

And how could she stand to watch him do it for the rest of her life?

Jarod's lithe form blurred in front of her. All the colors and the lights blended into the little cloud of dust rising from the arena floor. It could be this way for the rest of her life.

Where had that thought come from?

From her heart. From the very depths of her soul.

Tears stung in her eyes and she blinked; Jarod was sharp and clear now, irresistibly handsome as he held out his hand to accept Billy's congratulations. She stared at him, unable to move. It had been inevitable since the moment she met him and now it was irrevocable. She was in love with him.

The drive back to Tulsa was a quiet one. Jarod wasn't inclined to make conversation; he seemed to be still caught up in his own remote world. And she couldn't talk because she was listening to the din inside her head, trying to make some sense of the total confusion created by so many frightening new thoughts and feelings.

She couldn't actually fall in love with him, she told herself desperately. She simply couldn't. Nothing about their life-styles meshed. Sabrina was an outsider in the midst of the family that meant so much to him, and couldn't bear to think about his work, which obviously was his first love. How could they possibly have any kind of long-term relationship?

She was vaguely conscious that they were arriving back in town when they left the expressway, but he was turning the pickup into the parking lot at the store before she became aware of her exact surroundings. He was taking her to his apartment.

Her throat tightened. Not now. Not tonight. She had to get away somewhere by herself so she could think. As soon as she'd realized the depth of her feelings for him—the extent of the danger she was in—she'd been aching to be alone. She needed the space. And she needed time.

"I guess I forgot to mention it, but I need to go home now," she said, trying to make her tone light. "After all, it is almost one in the morning."

He shot her a swift glance. He was already parking the truck, but now he let the motor run.

"You mean you don't want to go to work? What was all that hassle I've been getting for the past two days about how much you need to get to the store?" His tone was teasing but the levity didn't touch his eyes.

She tried to smile, but her lips trembled. Darn! She didn't want him to be funny or remind her of the camaraderie that had always been between them. She didn't want him to look so duskily handsome in the slanting beam of the streetlight.

"I'll work tomorrow," she said shakily.

He was silent, watching her.

She tried to say something else, but she couldn't.

"Sabrina..."

The way he spoke her name tortured her, made her want to reach for him. All she had to do was hold out her hand and they'd walk inside with their arms around each other, their bodies brushing together; they'd make love all night long and...

And tomorrow he'd be gone. Gone to risk his life twice a day for weeks on end, gone to be absorbed into a strange, violent world that scared her to death, a world that he loved. He'd be gone and all her loneliness would be back, stronger than ever.

She stared straight ahead through the windshield at the white wall of the store, seeing Jarod's face as it had looked during his ride on the bull, then remembering it as he'd sat talking with Ridge and Billy under the hackberry tree. The visceral sense of separation shot through her again. She didn't belong with him. She'd been a fool to ever think that she did.

But she loved him. That fact overcame all the reasons why she shouldn't.

"Jarod, I really just want to go home alone tonight," she blurted. "There're so many things I need to think about.... I'm so confused...."

She swung her eyes to his at last. "You understand...."

He was staring at her, surprised, but a little wary, too. "I'm leaving tomorrow. This time it'll be at least a month, maybe even longer, before I work in a trip home."

She couldn't answer. She tried, but the panic was pushing at her too hard.

His narrowed eyes questioned her, pierced her, held her as if he were a hunter and she his prey.

She looked away and swallowed hard, trying to find words for the feelings that were pounding her.

He straightened abruptly, a proud set coming into his shoulders. "Well, I sure don't intend to beg you."

He jerked the truck into reverse and backed it out.

"I don't want you to beg me," she cried. "That's not what I . . ."

"Don't bother trying to explain," he growled savagely. He jammed the accelerator down and sped out into the almost empty street.

"Jarod, listen to me! I'm really mixed up right now and I need some time to think." The words were pouring out of her now, unconsidered, unbidden, trying to make some kind of order of the churning chaos of her emotions. "I'm not sure we should even keep on seeing each other. . . ."

"Well, this is a hell of a time to start making a decision like that!" His face closed to her completely. "Now you're back on your own turf and you're 'wanting to go home alone.'" The driving sarcasm made his voice even deeper. "You've really been wanting to do that ever since last night, haven't you? Ever since you had to spend a miserable evening with my family. Isn't that right?"

"No! That isn't true!"

"Don't lie to me, Sabrina." The words came slowly, bitterly from between the hard lines of his lips. "I saw how quiet you were at Darlene's house, and tonight at the rodeo you were stiff as a statue."

"I was scared! I was terrified you'd be hurt. I couldn't even breathe while you were riding."

"Well, for somebody who was scared breathless that I'd get hurt you're not worried about me now. I guess as soon as I got my feet back on the ground all the excitement was gone."

She felt her cheeks flush with angry frustration. "The excitement *isn't* gone! It's too much. I have to have a chance to..."

He shook his head. His low, bitter chuckle stopped her. "I've been so stupid. I should've known."

"Should've known what?"

"I should've known enough not to make a fool of myself twice. I learned a long time ago that women like you think you're too good for my kind of life. You're used to old mansions like your parents' house and country clubs and big fancy parties, and tearing your condo apart because you don't like the color of the kitchen tiles and whatever the hell else it is that the cream of Tulsa society indulges itself in."

"Jarod!" She was stunned by his outburst. "That isn't the problem at all."

He squealed into the turn and drove very fast up her mother's driveway. He stopped the truck in the exact spot he'd parked in before and cut the motor, then turned to face her. His eyes were as opaque as painted glass.

"I guess what trapped me this time was your cute little routine about wanting to play Indian." His stare bored into her thoughtfully. "Well, now I've learned. It won't happen again."

"But, Jarod, you don't know..."

Deliberately he turned away and got out of the truck, moving in a constrained way that made his anger seem even stronger. He came around and opened her door.

"I know that my family isn't good enough for you and I'm not good enough for yours. You didn't fool me for a minute the other night at Chi-Chi's. You were doing everything you could to keep your brother from seeing you with me."

She sat frozen to her seat, horrified. "Jarod, you've misunderstood! I didn't want you to meet Martin—"

"I know you didn't," he interrupted viciously, gesturing for her to get out. "*I* just told *you* that, remember?"

He put his hand behind her back, but he didn't touch her as he began walking her uncompromisingly up the steps.

She tried again. "But, Jarod, listen. I said..."

"You said you think we shouldn't keep on seeing each other," he said coldly. "It's too late now to do anything else about the store, but as far as our personal lives are concerned, I can certainly oblige you."

He turned and left her standing at the door.

She let herself into the store the next morning just before full daylight, but instead of going to her office she turned down the hallway to Jarod's apartment. She had to talk to him; this time she would *make* him listen.

At the door she raised her hand to knock and then hesitated, the memory of his last harsh words holding her knuckles away from the sleek, polished wood. He'd jumped to conclusions, and hadn't even tried to understand her....

He *had* to understand her, she thought fiercely. There had to be some kind of conciliation between them before he went back on the road. Last night had been the most wretchedly miserable one of her life. There was no way she could survive a whole month or more like that.

There was a long silence after she knocked. The sound reverberated in the empty building and for a moment she thought he wasn't at home. Then she heard his voice, low and rough.

"It's open."

She pushed at the heavy door and followed it inward.

He was lying on the sofa, propped up against one arm of it, his face a smoldering darkness against the white cushions. He didn't move.

"Jarod, I need to talk with you."

His only response was to settle the heel of his incredibly worn boot a little deeper into the soft cushions.

She came a few steps closer. His face was haggard, his thick hair disheveled as if he'd been raking his fingers through it. He'd been awake all night, too.

"Jarod, we can't go on for a month like this. We have to get something settled before you go."

He shifted the mug of steaming coffee that he was holding against his hard, bronzed belly. It clinked faintly on the silver belt buckle low on his waist.

"We settled it."

She tried to keep her eyes away from his hands, from his chest that was exposed by the blue work shirt swinging open on his shoulders. "No, we didn't. You walked away."

"Damn straight. As you pointed out, we've got some very basic cultural differences separating us, and it's about time we recognized that."

"I didn't say that, you . . ."

"You said that without ever opening your mouth, Ms. Dante," he drawled coldly. "The expressions on your face and the way you acted during our recent visit to the 'reservation' were pictures worth far more than a thousand words."

Tears sprang to her eyes and she turned to go, determined not to let him see them. The implacable wall of his stubbornness was too thick, too much for her to cope with in her upset state.

But at the open door she turned, driven to hurl one last weapon against it. "I don't care what you believe," she cried, "you're wrong. I love you, Jarod Redfeather. I love you!"

She stared into his eyes, astounded by the words. She hadn't even known she was going to say them; they'd been torn from her very soul.

He looked back at her, directly into her eyes, but his face was totally impassive. Above the high, hard cheekbones his eyes were opaque black bits of obsidian.

She didn't know how she got back to her office, but she huddled there all morning, her blood like ice. She told Dorothy and Zelda to function as if she weren't in, and she kept the door firmly closed, staring off into space while she tried to find the keys to the puzzle. Suddenly, in the space of a heartbeat, on the strength of one request from her to be taken home, Jarod had decided that she was a terrible snob and that the differences between them were irreconcilable.

And they *were*. They didn't have a chance. Not so long as he refused to talk to her and tell her what she had done or said to make him think those things.

The blast of a horn very close outside startled her. She got up and went to the window. A yellow cab was waiting by the side entrance; while she watched, Jarod came out to meet it. He was entirely different from the way he'd looked in his apartment just a few hours earlier: he was dressed in crisply pressed jeans and a jean jacket open over a plaid shirt; his boots and hat were expensive and immaculate.

He swung his rigging bag and a backpack onto the seat with swift, economical movement, then got in after them, sweeping off his hat to keep it from brushing the ceiling of the car. He was a coolly professional cowboy with places to go and appointments to keep—*he* certainly wasn't lying around curled into the fetal position because of worry over *her*.

She watched the cab disappear, through tears that she wouldn't let fall. Well, if he could do that, so could she. She'd stop this insane moping, get back to work and forget that Jarod Redfeather was ever anything more than the name on the sign in front of the store.

She turned from the window and walked to her desk. This entire experience with him had been an interesting episode in her life, but it was all over. The whole world knew it wasn't smart to get romantically involved at work. She should consider it a blessing that it was over. From now on he was the owner and she was the manager. Period.

The phone on her desk shrilled and she let it ring, willing it to drown out the hurting cry inside her. After twenty-eight years she'd found the one man who could set free all the riotous feeling that was in her and now he was gone.

Chapter Ten

Sabrina pulled into her parking space, turned off the motor and took the keys from the ignition. But then, instead of getting out and rushing into her office as she had been doing every day and almost every evening for the past three weeks, she just sat.

She glanced at the carved wooden sign that read Jarod Redfeather; it was swinging gently back and forth in the early-morning breeze. She read the words over and over again, trying each time to think of the store and not the man. She had to forget that anything had ever been between them. He was simply the owner of this place where she worked and she was his employee.

She tore her eyes away from his name and looked around her, deliberately forcing her thoughts to the day at hand. Slowly she rolled down the window so the car wouldn't later explode in the blistering sun. The air was already heavy and warm; by noon it would be so hot that the pavement of the parking lot would be broiling. Would that keep customers away?

Her glance moved up to the cloth banner billowing from the ends of the ceiling beams at the top of the white stucco wall. Open Today, it announced in big brown letters. Official Grand Opening Celebration Friday, August 16. Come in for a Buggy Ride. Watch the Green Country Square Dancers. Have a cold drink and . . .

Darn. She had to call again and confirm the deal about the buggy rides. For some reason she'd been putting it off.

Because she didn't want to think about the grand opening celebration, a tiny voice inside her suggested. Jarod would be back for that and he was the last thing on earth she could handle right now. She'd barely been able to talk to him on the phone while they made the plans for the colorful event he wanted. Evidently he hoped the grand opening would be a real party—a gathering of all the family and friends he'd ever known—and the thought of coping with that while trying to accustom herself to the fact that their personal relationship was over was just too much.

Sabrina jerked the car door open and got out. There were a million things for her to do today and she might as well get to them. They would be open to customers for a ten-day trial period before the official grand opening, and those would probably be the ten busiest days of all.

Zelda's greeting confirmed that. She barely said hello before launching into a recital of the most urgent messages for Sabrina.

"Two of the new hires called to say they don't want the job after all, and Dorothy said to tell you that another one didn't show. Also, Lawrence was in here a minute ago asking whether we have any more display racks for hats. There aren't enough out there to make the kind of arrangement you wanted."

Sabrina forced her mind to start functioning. "There are some more in the storeroom. Lawrence ought to know that."

"He probably just forgot," Zelda said cheerfully. "Everybody's so excited about finally having customers that they're rushing around like crazy." She made herself a note at the bottom of a page that was already full of jottings. "I'll tell him."

"Remind him that it's only an hour and a half until those customers come in, too," Sabrina said sharply. "He should've had that display done last night."

Zelda nodded and went back to her list. "Mrs. Howard just called. She'll be in before nine to arrange the plants. She can't hang the Navaho rugs because they haven't come in yet. She said to assure you that she'd have them before the day of the grand opening."

"Well, I certainly hope so," Sabrina muttered.

Zelda glanced up quizzically at her unaccustomed disgruntled tone, then began reading again. "Your brother called yesterday afternoon just after you left. He'll come by late today with the supplement to your software package."

"Ask him to bring us a program that'll make the computer sell boots," Sabrina grumbled. "If we have a lot of customers today we're going to be in real trouble."

"I've already called Temporary Personnel." Zelda looked at her worriedly. "It'll be all right, Ms. Dante. Don't be nervous."

Good heavens, Sabrina chastised herself. Who's the leader around here, anyway? If this keeps up the whole staff will be snarling at the customers before the morning is over.

Giving Zelda a tight smile she went into her office. You have to get a grip on yourself, she thought fiercely. Stop thinking about Jarod and ten days from now, and concentrate on today.

"And Mrs. Kelly," Zelda's litany continued from the doorway. "I wasn't able to find her at home yesterday, but I'll try again this morning."

"Not too early," Sabrina said. "She's a true lady of leisure; she's never up before noon. If we're going to sell her a painting we don't want to wake her up to talk to her about it."

She poured herself a cup of coffee and then settled into the chair behind her desk.

"Which painting is that? Have I seen it?" Zelda dropped into the leather wing chair, apparently relieved that Sabrina was sounding more like herself.

"Not yet. It's one that—" consciously she avoided using Jarod's name "—that Angie Fourkiller has done. It's a study of a mother and child on the Trail of Tears. Lucille Kelly has a stunning collection of art that portrays mother and child, from all over the world, and this would be a perfect addition to it."

"Are we going to display it, even if Mrs. Kelly buys it?"

"I hope so. I'll call Angie today after I talk to Lucille. I want it here at least for the grand opening. If I can start Lucille thinking and talking about it, it'll be a big boost for Angie's career, plus it'll bring in a lot of people for the big celebration."

A lot of people she knew, she thought, as she sipped at the coffee. At least she'd have somebody to talk to and that would help keep her mind off Jarod.

She straightened up and squared her shoulders resolutely. "Bring me the letters you typed yesterday, Zelda," she said, "and when I've signed them I'm off to the front lines. When Mrs. Howard arrives, I'll be in the art department."

The day was just as hectic as Sabrina had anticipated, and after she got into it, she was glad. She didn't have time to think about anything except the problems at hand; she took time out from working directly with her personnel and the customers only to finish up with Madge Howard and to make the phone calls to Lucille Kelly and to Angie.

Lucille was excited about Sabrina's description of the work and practically committed herself to buying it on her recommendation. She promised to come to the grand opening to see it and meet the artist, and Sabrina hung up from the conversation feeling that Angie was truly on her way to building a following. Lucille and her daughter, Brenda Tate, were active on many Tulsa committees involving the arts and they were never shy about touting their favorites.

Sabrina smiled as she dialed Angie's number. This news would bring out the enthusiasm she'd hoped for the first time she'd called her. She was sure of it.

But Angie wasn't happy when Sabrina gave her the news. She seemed . . . wary, Sabrina thought, puzzled, as she tried to put a name to the feeling vibrating over the telephone wires. No, she sounded almost offended. Or scared.

"You *sold* it?"

"Well, it isn't absolutely definite yet, but Mrs. Kelly trusts my judgment, and the subject of the painting is one that she's built a huge collection around. It's as good as sold, because I know that when she sees it she's going to love it."

Angie was silent.

Sabrina frowned at the telephone. What was it with this child? The first time she'd met her she'd seemed thrilled that Sabrina liked her work. But ever since she'd been trying to help her make a real career, she'd been totally uncooperative.

"Angie, this could be your big chance," Sabrina said impatiently. "Mrs. Kelly can bring you lots more sales and recognition by the right people...."

"She's collecting paintings about the Trail of Tears?" Angie interrupted faintly.

"No, of mothers and children. Art with a Madonna theme. *Triumphal Journey* is perfect for her."

Zelda appeared in the doorway to signal that someone wanted to see her, and Sabrina nodded.

"Angie, I have to go," she said hurriedly. "I just need the painting as soon as possible. By a week from Friday at the latest. That's the grand opening day— you can just bring it with you when you come. You will be coming for the party, won't you?"

Again, silence.

"Angie, you are coming?"

"Yes."

"Good. See you then!"

Zelda was in the room before she could replace the receiver. "Who is it, Zelda?"

"It's Lawrence. He says the air-conditioning system just quit."

They sweltered through the long afternoon while Zelda made urgent calls for repairmen and Sabrina wished she'd never robbed the maintenance budget. By the time help arrived and cool air was circulating again, very few customers were left. The nerves of the staff were completely on edge. Sabrina wandered through the store announcing that everything was under control again, trying to lift morale with a smile here, a comment there.

Then she stepped out onto the sidewalk to close the double glass doors, and the fierceness of the heat almost took her breath. What a laugh, she thought, staring at the traffic moving in four crowded lanes down Memorial. It was the funniest thing in the world for her to be going around saying everything was under control. She'd never felt so tautly strung, so nearly *out* of control in her life.

Sabrina stood there in the building sunlight for a moment, wishing to be someplace cool and quiet, and hating to go back inside the store. If she had to face one more problem or ignore one more reminder of Jarod she would run out the door and go screaming down the street, traffic or no traffic.

She thought of the peaceful serenity of her new home, the home she'd had time only to sleep in during these recent frantic days. That was all she wanted, she thought. She longed to go there, to crawl into the dim, cool cavern of her own place and simply forget about Jarod, her job and every problem connected with them both.

"Well, I've heard of not having sense enough to come in out of the rain, but you're the first person I've met who didn't have sense enough to come in out of the sun!"

She turned. Martin was walking along the sidewalk, as crisp and cool looking as if the thermometer read 72 instead of 102. She hadn't even noticed his car.

"Hey, what is this, anyway?" he continued to tease as he reached her. "The first day you're open for customers and you're standing around meditating instead of selling out the store?''

She met his eyes and tried to smile. "It seemed like a good idea at the time."

He took her arm. "Now I know the sun's gotten to you. I never thought I'd hear a remark like that from my dedicated, career-minded sister! You'd better let me escort you back to work."

The warmth in his voice and the touch of his hand were so comforting that they stripped away her thin defenses. She should be wearing a button that said "I need a hug," she thought wryly. She wanted to lay her head on his chest and cry.

"You may escort me anywhere *except* back to work," she said, trying to match the lightness of his tone. Her voice broke, though, on the last word, and she turned away.

"Sabrina?"

He took her shoulders and swung her around to face him. She stared at his immaculate white shirtfront, afraid to meet his gaze. The nervous strength that had carried her through the day was draining away, leaving her defenseless. It was as if a tightly wound wire of tension had pulled her deep into her work during all the days since Jarod had left and held her there. Until she got the store in shape to open, she'd been too busy to feel the loneliness. Well, now it was open. Her brother was with her, sympathetic and concerned, and the wire was coming unwound.

But she couldn't talk to Martin. Not about Jarod. At the moment she was entirely too vulnerable to defend her foolish involvement with him or to deal with a big brotherly "I told you so."

Martin was shaking her gently. "Sabrina, what's wrong? What's happened?"

She took a deep, ragged breath and raised her eyes so Martin's face would blot out the image of Jarod's.

"Oh, hardly anything," she said bitterly. "We just started the day three clerks and two hat racks short and everything's gone downhill from there. The air conditioner quit and it got as hot inside the store as it is out here, so all the customers left. The new ones drove up and saw the doors standing open and just kept on going." She swallowed hard. "I called the people who'd installed the system, and..."

He stopped the rush of words with a chuckle. "I have never, in all my thirty-seven years, seen anyone so upset over an air conditioner." He was still trying for the teasing tone, but his voice held an underlying concern now, and his eyes were worried.

"Little sister, I'm afraid there's something you aren't telling me. You're about to fall apart."

She pulled away. "No, I'm fine. I just need to get away for a while." Distractedly she tightened the clasp that held her hair away from her face. "I think I'll go home. Why don't you follow me there and we'll talk about the software over a cold lemonade?"

"I have a better idea. Come to my place and I'll give you a nice, cold wine and some dinner." He reached for her hand and pulled it through his arm. "You'll love it," he promised. "The air conditioner's working fine; I can set it down to sixty degrees if you want."

She laughed shakily. "You've talked me into it. That's the best offer I've had all day."

She sat at the breakfast bar, sipping from a glass of chilled white wine, watching Martin move around the kitchen putting eggs on to boil and taking cold ham and a variety of fresh vegetables and fruits from the refrigerator.

She ought to do something to help, she thought, but she didn't have the energy to move a finger.

He sensed that, just as he had known that she was hiding the real reason for her emotions being in shambles.

"No, no, there isn't a thing you can do," he teased, pretending that she'd offered. "You just sit right there and collect your thoughts." He tossed an impish grin over his shoulder as he began tearing lettuce leaves. "And when they're all in one basket, I'll be happy to hear them."

He made an occasional remark about his day or about his running or the food he was preparing, but most of the time there was a companionable silence between them. His pleasant company and the wine worked insidiously against her resolve not to talk to him about Jarod, and finally, almost before she'd realized she was going to speak, the whole story began to pour out.

She was absorbed in it, in trying to find a clue to Jarod's confusing anger that had destroyed them so abruptly, in trying to rid herself of her loneliness in the telling of it. But on another level she was aware of her brother, too, and of the fact that he was listening with his total self to every word she spoke.

She looked up as she finished and saw that he was standing completely still at the counter, the vegetables forgotten on the cutting board in front of him. "So," she concluded with a despairing little shrug, "you can go ahead and say 'I told you so.' You were absolutely right when you warned me against him in the first place."

He looked at her. For a long minute the room was very quiet. Then he shook his head. "No. I was absolutely wrong."

She felt her eyes widen in astonishment. "Martin! What are you talking about?"

"I'm talking about some new brotherly advice, a word of wisdom much more valid than any I've given you yet. Are you listening?"

She nodded.

"Stop moping around here and go get him."

"Go get . . . Jarod?"

"Jarod. Don't let it end this way."

Shocked surprise and a tiny glimmer of hope rippled through her. She thrust the hope away, angry that he'd created it.

"Whatever happened to the old 'find somebody from your own world' routine?"

"Nobody from your own world ever made you feel like this," he answered flatly. "Babe, you love this Redfeather guy. You don't have any choice."

"Oh, yes, I do. I have the choice of forgetting he ever existed. I'll get this store on its feet, stay long enough for this job to be credible on my résumé and then move on to whatever's next in my life."

He shook his head wisely. "You'll never forget him."

He crossed to the bar and leaned on it, directly across from her so that he could look into her eyes to emphasize his words.

"Sabrina, I've dated a lot of women, but I've never felt the way you're feeling right now about any of them." Gently he reached for her hand. "I only wish I could. That's what I'm looking for. That's what the whole *world* is looking for. You've got a chance at it, little sister. It'd be a sin to let it slip away."

"But we're too different. We don't understand each other. You've told me that from the very beginning and now I know that it's true. Everything that happened just before he left proves it."

He smiled at her and, even in her misery, she was struck by the love in his eyes. "You two can work it out," he said reassuringly.

She pushed the wordless hope away from her again. She felt tears spring to her lashes. "No. No. He's different, Martin. He's an Indian. He's stoic; he never talks about feelings. He keeps everything buried inside."

He wagged his head in mock despair. "Now who's stereotyping? I seem to remember that only a few weeks ago you were jumping all over me for doing that very thing."

"It's not stereotyping—it's the truth! He won't talk things out with me or explain any of his feelings. He'll never tell me why sometimes he turns so cold and distant without any warning. This bewildering anger over my snobbishness, or whatever it is that he's imagining about me, is the first emotion he's ever talked about; in fact, it's the first real emotion he's ever shown toward me!"

He questioned that statement with a wry lift of one eyebrow.

She felt a blush spread into her cheeks. "Well . . . I mean, in words. He . . . he's never said that he loves me."

"Well, sometimes that takes a while."

She shrugged hopelessly. "Yeah. Like forever."

"First you may have to tell him that you love him."

"I did," she admitted. "But it was written all over his face that he didn't believe me."

"Tell him again. *Make* him believe you."

She just looked at him, letting the frustrated question of how to do that show in her face.

"All I know is that if I ever saw a look in a woman's eyes like the one that comes into yours when you talk about him, I'd be hooked forever," he told her. "He will be, too."

She sat very still, listening to him now in the same intense way he'd listened to her. With every word he uttered, that tiny, stubborn hope deep inside her was growing a little larger.

He walked around the bar and took the stool next to hers. "Look at it this way, sis, you did put him down pretty hard. You were just thinking about needing a little time to get your head together but to Jarod that simple request to be taken home looked like sudden and total rejection.''

"But I didn't mean—"

"He doesn't know what you meant," he interrupted, holding her eye firmly. "After all, you did say that you were thinking of not seeing him anymore."

She nodded glumly. "Now I could cut out my tongue."

He smiled in sympathy. "Why don't you use it to talk to him instead? You're the one who'll have to make the first move now."

"I can't. I absolutely can't."

He whirled on the stool and reached for the wine bottle. "You absolutely can't go on in the state you're in," he declared flatly. "And you know that. Now, have another glass of wine and let me tell you exactly what you should do."

By the time she let herself into her own place later that night Sabrina was filled with a crazy sense of hope that Martin might be right. She *would* try again to talk to Jarod, she decided. Four weeks had gone by and the heat of his anger was past.

But after she'd showered and climbed into bed she lay for a long time looking at the ceiling, seeing the image of Jarod's scornful face when she'd told him she loved him. She didn't have the faintest idea of how to get past those defenses and win his trust. She closed her eyes to shut out the picture, but sleep wouldn't come.

The day before the grand opening celebration was much quieter than she had expected. Every detail about the horses and buggy rides, the refreshments and door prizes had been taken care of. Sabrina hated that. She needed bustling excitement and constant demands on her time to blot out the thought of Jarod's return. He'd be back sometime that night. Would she have the courage to talk to him as she'd told Martin she would?

Yes, she decided, as she wandered through the store during the afternoon. She didn't have a choice. No matter what the outcome, she had to try.

She inspected the appearance of each department and made sure that everyone knew what to do during the next day's big event. Madge Howard was there to hang the Navaho rugs that had finally arrived, and Sabrina spent a few minutes talking with her, then went back to her office.

Five minutes later, Jarod stormed in. "What the *hell* is going on around here?"

She looked up from the papers on her desk, her heart constricting at the sight of him. He was looming in the doorway, filling it, his bags still in his hand.

"I just talked to a woman out there who's hanging fifty-thousand dollars' worth of hand-loomed Navaho rugs on the wall," he went on, without giving her a chance to reply. "She introduced herself as Madge Howard, our interior decorator."

"Then, no doubt, that is exactly who she is," Sabrina answered sarcastically.

"I don't give a damn who she is," he snapped, advancing into the room like a vengeful general at the head of his troops. "What I want to know is how she got hired to work here. We agreed a long time ago that there was no money in the budget for decorators."

"No, we didn't. You said that. I said I would look for some, and I found it."

"You couldn't have. It wasn't there."

She took a deep breath. She might as well tell him now. The crisis with the air-conditioning was past with no damage done, and the amount she allotted for maintenance would probably be sufficient for the year.

"I took it out of maintenance."

"Maintenance!"

He dropped the bags into the wing chair and bent over her desk, his eyes blazing. "Of all the stupid, harebrained ideas! You can't take it out of maintenance! What if we had an emergency?"

"We did have one with the air conditioner, but most of it was covered by the warranty. A lot of the other machinery is, too, since it's so new."

"And if something happens that isn't covered? What do you plan to do then?"

His overbearing arrogance was too much to bear; it created a fury in her that destroyed her self-control in one swift stroke. "Pay for it out of my own pocket!" she snapped, standing up to face him.

His mouth tightened and his lips went white. "You keep your money out of this," he snarled. "I should've known if I hired a spoiled rich girl who's never heard of a limited budget that this is what I'd get.''

He turned away and paced to the window. ''I don't know how you ever got as far as you did in San Francisco.''

''I got as far as I did because I was good at my job and I worked like a slave at it.'' She flung the words at his broad back.

He whirled. ''You got as far as you did because your name is Dante and your family has influence all over this country. People like you all hang together. Always.''

His eyes burned into hers. She had never seen him so angry. ''And people like you also think that any problem can be solved with money. I learned that when I graduated from high school thinking that I was going to college with the girl I loved, that I was going to marry her. But her parents didn't want her married to a poor, low-down Indian. They corrected that little situation by giving her a Jaguar to drive and a trip to Europe and offering me a free education. She took it—I didn't.''

He crossed to the chair in two long strides and picked up his bags. ''You're all alike, Sabrina. You and Diane Medford could be twins.'' His black eyes bored into her, through her. ''Don't *ever* pay for anything around here out of your pocket,'' he warned. ''I don't intend to be obligated to you in any way.''

He slammed the door shut behind him. She slumped into her chair, stunned. Her whole body throbbed with hurt as if she'd been physically beaten. The anger and frustration swirling in her stomach only made it worse.

Martin was wrong, she thought. She couldn't reach Jarod again.

She'd never even reached him to begin with, she realized then, with a little frisson of pure despair. He'd never seen her solely as herself. That unseen standard he'd been judging her by was another woman, someone who'd hurt him in the past. From the minute he'd seen her mother's house he'd stereotyped her as another Diane Medford.

His accusing voice still rang in her ears. "People like you..."

She ran her fingers into her hair and massaged her throbbing temples. She'd never had a fair chance with him from the start.

Chapter Eleven

"They're waiting for you out front, Ms. Dante,"
Zelda said as she hurried up to Sabrina. "Mr. Redfeather said to tell you that the videotaping crew is
here."

The knot in Sabrina's stomach tightened. She didn't
want to go out front. She couldn't see or talk with
anybody, much less be the charming, professional
store manager for the lens of a camera.

And she was unable to face Jarod.

Her hand trembled under the heavy squash-blossom
necklace she was adding to the display. She couldn't
see him without pouring out the angry despair that
filled her.

But she must not let herself do that, she thought fiercely as she settled the necklace over the saddle horn. It would be as useless as the last time she'd tried. Words would never get through to Jarod now. The hardness in his eyes and the granite set of his face as he'd slammed out of her office had told her that.

"Ms. Dante?"

Sabrina sighed. "I'm going in a minute, Zelda. I'm nearly finished with this."

She stepped back to look at the effect. The saddle lay sideways on a Navaho rug; some Cherokee baskets spilling still more turquoise and silver were mixed with pots of yellow and bronze chrysanthemums around it.

"That looks great!" Zelda approved.

She glanced back at Sabrina. "And so do you. Your idea about wearing that dress was wonderful; it's the very best way to advertise it."

"Thanks. I'm just not too sure about how I *feel* in it."

"You should feel like the model of the year," Zelda said firmly. She came closer to examine the beadwork on Molly's creation. "I love it! How many of them did you get?"

"Just this one so far. Molly hasn't finished any others."

"Well, then, if anyone wants to buy it today, don't let them. Tell them it's not for sale until I can save up my money."

Sabrina chuckled in spite of the tension pulling at her. "Zelda, we're trying to *sell* things, not keep them."

She leaned forward and pulled at a fold in the rug, moving one of the baskets to a slightly more interesting position.

The secretary glanced at her watch. "I hate to say this..."

"I know. I really am going."

She picked up her clipboard and glanced at it. "Zelda, would you call Angie Fourkiller and ask her what time she's coming today? I want to be sure that her painting is here when Lucille Kelly comes in to see it."

"All right."

"And come find me when the buggy-ride man arrives."

"Will do," Zelda said, going off in the direction of the office.

Sabrina lingered in front of the display, making sure that it was perfect. She'd created it herself early that morning in spite of the myriad last-minute details she'd had to take care of.

And in spite of the facts that Madge had done a great job and that she also had a perfectly competent window dresser. She shook her head ruefully. They'd both hate her for it, but she'd had to do something *visible*.

Something to show to that arrogant man, she admitted bitterly as she turned away from it. She'd had to have some evidence, no matter how small, that he'd been wrong about the way she'd built her career.

She started toward the front door, but at the last minute she veered off into the powder room. She had to check the dress and her hair, she told herself. After all, she was going to be filmed this morning.

But mostly she had to pull herself together, another part of her admitted. She'd avoided Jarod the whole time she'd been at the store that morning, but she couldn't do so any longer. Now it was time for them to play the roles of genial cohosts for the widely advertised grand opening celebration.

What a laugh! she thought bitterly. The animosity crackling between them would probably drive all the guests and customers away.

She stared into the mirror, hardly seeing the reflection of her face or the supple suede dress, its fringed hem falling against her calves, which were encased in knee-high moccasins fastened with silver buttons. Absently she loosened her hair, letting it fall straight to the beaded shoulders of the dress and over the tops of her bare arms; then she bent to pull one of the moccasins up more firmly. She adjusted the tie at the top of it and fiddled with one of the buttons for a minute.

Finally she straightened and drew in a deeply ragged breath. She left the room, headed for the front door and the camera crew. And Jarod.

In spite of all her efforts at control, her pulse quickened as she caught a glimpse of him, handsomely dressed and hatted, pacing back and forth just outside the entryway. He turned when she opened the door.

His implacable eyes took her in all at once, widening almost imperceptibly as he absorbed the dress and moccasins, then narrowing again. "Good morning."

She half expected him to add, "Ms. Dante." His greeting was so formally polite.

Resentment swept through her at his impersonal tone, but she managed to imitate it. "Good morning."

Deliberately she turned to the advertising director, Virgil Fox. "Hello. How are you today?"

"Great!" he exclaimed with the exaggerated cheerfulness that was his trademark. "Absolutely fabulous! Now, we want to get some shots of the two of you opening the doors," he said. "And later maybe a few of you riding in a horse-drawn buggy. There'll be so much going on around here today we'll have material for several tremendous commercials."

Oh, no, she thought, as he went on to expound on his plans in greater detail. The filming would be just one more force that would throw her and Jarod together; it would be hard to escape. Well, at least she could see to it that they were surrounded by people. She never wanted to be alone with him again.

But the next moment she was wishing that the two of them could be magically transported to his hilltop cabin, or to her "extravagant" condo—to any place at all where they could be hidden from the world and she could try to make him see that she was not Diane Medford. They were standing close together at the director's urging and the instinctive desire to reach for his hand, to touch his arm, to tilt her face up for his kiss was brutally strong.

Then the cheery little man told Jarod to look at her.

His eyes bored into hers. A sardonic little smile curled the corners of his mouth. "Really throwing yourself into the act, aren't you?" he muttered tightly, indicating her costume with a quick gesture. "No high heels or business suits today—just one of the down-home folks for the big occasion."

Her desire disappeared in one hot flame of anger. "I had a new idea for making the store a success," she told him in a sweetly sarcastic tone. "This time I'm exploiting my Indian blood instead of my name. I'm just trying to put a little variety into my career. It gets so boring, otherwise."

"As boring as contradicting your boss's orders?"

"I did *not* contradict your orders. We had an agreement. If you'll just stop and think..."

"Face me and smile, please," Virgil interrupted happily. "Great! Now, Sabrina, if you'll do the honor of cutting the ribbon..."

She moved through the rest of the formalities at Jarod's side, but there was no opportunity to talk to him again. Some of their special guests arrived, including a reporter from the business page of the afternoon newspaper, and they all went inside to look around the store and have coffee and tiny cinnamon and sausage rolls from the long festive table set up in the foyer.

They were just finishing the last questions of the interview when Martin came in.

"I hardly recognized you!" he said, taking Sabrina's hand and twirling her around. "For a moment I thought for sure it was Sacajawea or Pocahontas."

"Neither one of them was Cherokee," Jarod said, turning from saying goodbye to the reporter to greet Martin with a handshake. "How's it going?"

"Fine." Martin smiled at him warmly.

Sabrina asked, "Jarod, you remember Martin, my brother?"

"Of course." He glanced at her, then back at Martin. The thought of her hesitating to introduce them still rankled.

"Sabrina tells me you run," he said with a cordiality that amazed her. "How's your time?"

That started an involved discussion of times and places to run, training methods, diets and shoes. Sabrina stood listening to them, completely amazed by how well they got on.

When Jarod mentioned that many of the cowboys he knew did yoga in preparation for bull riding, Martin was fascinated and they began speculating as to whether that would be good for their running, too. They would have gone on all day, she thought, if Virgil hadn't reappeared and taken Jarod away.

Martin echoed her thought. "I guess it's a good thing we were interrupted," he said, glancing at his watch. "I was about to forget that I have to be all the way across town in half an hour."

"Oh, I wish you didn't have to go. *I* haven't had a chance to talk with you at all."

"Soon," he promised. He pulled her hand through his arm. "Come on, walk me to the car and I'll tell you how great your man is."

My man, she thought bleakly as she let him guide her through the customers going in and out of the doors. If only he knew.

At the car he took both her hands in his and smiled down at her. "He's a great guy, Sabrina. I like him. I can see why you feel the way you do about him."

Her throat tightened and she swallowed hard against the lump in it. Finally she managed to say, "I only wish I didn't feel that way."

"You two haven't had a chance to talk yet?"

"No." She longed to tell him the horrible story of Jarod's homecoming the day before, but there wasn't time. He had an appointment and she had the rest of the day to get through. She couldn't do that with her face blotched by tears.

"Well, you will," he said confidently, giving her hands a final squeeze before he swung into the car. "And then you'll be all set." He smiled up at her through the open window. "Look at it this way, sis: with me as your brother and Jarod as your favorite man you can't go wrong. Anybody can see that you have great taste."

She smiled back at him, unable to resist his teasing even in her misery. "You're the one who ought to be talking to him," she said. "You seem to get through to him a whole lot better than I do."

"You can do it," he assured her. "Just find the right time and then don't give up."

He started the motor. She stepped closer to the car; she could hardly let him leave. "Martin, he hasn't even given me a chance to try...." Her voice trailed off into nothingness.

His eyes darkened with concern and his smile faded. "Sabrina, remember what I've told you and don't give up," he told her emphatically. "You love this guy and you're going to make him know that. I know you are. My little sister can do anything."

"I wish," she whispered.

"You can," he repeated. "I have total faith in you."

The words tore at her heart. She squeezed his fingers, then moved back. "You'd better go or you'll be late," she said. "Thanks for the good words."

He smiled. "You're welcome. I'll be waiting for the progress report."

He waved and backed out of the space. She stood there until he disappeared into the traffic, then she turned back to the store.

Jarod was just inside the door, another cup of coffee in his hand, talking with a large man in Western clothes whom Sabrina recognized as Webb Talliaferro, a prominent local rancher. Immediately behind them, accepting coffee from the caterer's helper, was a sleek strawberry blonde who seemed vaguely familiar. When she turned Sabrina saw it was Brenda Tate.

"Sabrina!" Brenda's high voice carried, and Jarod and Mr. Talliaferro both turned to glance at her as Sabrina went to join her.

"Mother'll be by later," Brenda said. "I wanted to come with her, but I have an Arts Committee meeting this afternoon and there was just no way."

"I'm glad you came, no matter what time it is," Sabrina said. "It's good to see you again."

"And you, too!" Brenda's beautifully made-up eyes surveyed Sabrina thoroughly, taking in every detail of her beaded dress and moccasins. "I must say you do look a bit different nowadays, Sabrina."

Sabrina smiled. "I suppose so. I don't dress like this every day, but I may if I can ever get one of these for my own. It's the most comfortable *beautiful* thing I've ever worn."

Brenda continued to consider it. "That one isn't yours? You're selling them here?"

"That's right. We'll have a limited number. The beadwork is hand done and so is the stitching, so the woman who makes them can't turn them out *too* fast."

Brenda laughed. "Well, yes, and she probably doesn't rush herself any, either. You've heard all those jokes about Navaho Standard Time."

"This woman is Cherokee."

"Well, Cherokee Standard Time, then."

Sabrina felt Jarod move slightly behind her and she sensed a lull in his conversation with the rancher. Was he listening to her and Brenda? The word Cherokee had probably caught his attention.

Brenda sipped at her coffee, still considering the dress. "Well, Sabrina, who knows? Ethnic may be coming back in. You may just be in the forefront of the latest style," she said in a joking tone.

"I may be," Sabrina said dryly. She tried to think of a change of subject. "Would you like for me to show you around the store? Madge Howard decorated it and I think she did a terrific job."

"Oh, I'd love to, but I really don't have the time to look at boots and saddles and jeans and ropes and whatever else," Brenda said. "I just ran by to see this painting you were talking to Mother about. She's so excited about finding a new Indian artist right here under our very noses!"

"Oh, Brenda, I'm sorry, but the painting isn't here yet. I'm expecting it sometime around noon." Sabrina berated herself silently. Oh, *why* hadn't she called Angie last night and urged her to come early? If Brenda liked the painting she'd have told the Arts Committee all about it that afternoon.

Brenda pouted in disappointment. She glanced at her watch. "I just can't stay that long," she said. "After the Arts Committee I'm going to Margaret's to start planning the Opera Ball. You remember Margaret Blake, don't you?"

"Yes. How is she?"

"Great." Brenda put down her cup and looked back at Sabrina. "We want you to come to lunch with us sometime. And we need to get you involved in some of these committees and things, too," she said thoughtfully. "Mother tells me you're back in town to stay. Why don't you let me submit your name to..."

"Oh, Brenda, I can't. Today's a perfect example. You all are meeting this afternoon and I have to be here at the store."

"Have to?" Brenda questioned archly.

Sabrina winced and tried to move farther away from Jarod and his companion. He didn't need any more evidence for his "spoiled rich girl" stereotype of her.

"I enjoy working, Brenda," she said mildly. "My career..."

"But I'm talking about your social life, too!" Brenda exclaimed in her clearly audible voice. "You've always put your career ahead of everything else, and it isn't good for you! You've been a recluse ever since you got back. We haven't seen you at the club...."

A group of customers jostled them and Sabrina grasped the chance to glance at Jarod. He was closer to her than she thought, still with Talliaferro; they seemed to be sipping coffee more than they were talking.

As she watched, Zelda hurried up to give Jarod a message in which Sabrina caught the word "outside." Good, she thought. That would get him out of earshot of Brenda's chattering tongue.

She fended off Brenda's well-intended directions for a little while longer, agreed to have lunch with her and Margaret at a purposely vague date, then managed to ease her out the door. Sabrina took a few minutes to wander through the store, listening for comments from customers and checking to see that none of her employees needed assistance. The trial run seemed to be paying off: everything was running smoothly. Zelda found Sabrina in the art department wishing fervently that Angie and her painting would arrive before Lucille Kelly did.

"The buggy-ride man is here," she said. "He just drove up out front."

Sabrina thanked her and hurried out. She needed to be sure that the man had understood what she wanted; she also was going to tell Virgil to get some film of children and other customers enjoying the rides and petting the horses. That would make the liveliest commercial of the day. And probably the most useful one, she thought. If the rides proved to be popular she was going to arrange for them on a regular basis.

She spoke to the driver of the first buggy, the man with whom she'd made the arrangements, and they discussed the number of passengers and the length of each ride. He was eager to get his day's work started, so she went to help Dorothy organize a quickly growing crowd of eager children into two waiting lines before she tried to find Virgil.

The two buggies had just started their first trek when Jarod materialized beside her. "I need to talk to you," he barked. "Come over here."

He pulled her into the relative privacy created by a pillar of the entryway roof and a small tree.

She glared at him. "What are you doing? Can't you see that Dorothy needs some help over there?"

"She'll go get somebody else to help," he said impatiently. "Forget about her and listen to me. When you see Angie, don't say a word to her about *Triumphal Journey*."

She stared at him, completely astonished. "Why not? What are you talking about? Is she here? Did she bring it?"

"She's here, but she didn't bring it. She's over there in the car crying because she doesn't want to face you."

"*Me?*" Sabrina gasped, mystified. "Why not?"

"She said that you had Zelda call her again this morning to remind her to bring the painting and that you'd called about it several times before. Sabrina, the child doesn't want to sell that painting, so quit badgering her about it!"

She stared at him, not believing what she'd just heard. "I haven't been badgering her about it! She agreed to sell the painting. Jarod, she's never said one word about wanting to keep it!"

"Well, she does want to keep it, and she damn well has a right to. Don't mention it to her again."

"But *why*? Why did she lead me on like this if she never wanted to sell it in the first place?"

"Because..."

A raucous rebel yell rose over the sound of the band and his eyes flicked away from her to the entryway. "I'll explain later," he said abruptly. "Here's some boys I've got to see."

He moved away, then stopped. "Don't ask Angie about this," he repeated. "I'll explain later."

He stepped out into view and into the handshakes and backslaps of four or five young cowboys.

"Hey, Redfeather," one of them shouted. "What kind of place is this, anyhow? You give credit to broken-down saddle bums like ol' Kevin here?"

"You bet," Jarod answered jovially. "All he has to do is sign over half of his winnings."

A general laugh, louder than the yell, greeted that remark. "You're gonna go flat broke, then," another one shouted. "Half of *his* winnin's is half of nothin'!"

They surged on into the store, laughing and talking. Sabrina stood looking after them. Nobody else seemed to have any trouble communicating with Jarod, she thought; *she* was evidently the only one on a completely different wavelength.

A wave of despondency washed over her and she slumped against the pillar. He'd changed like a chameleon when he'd stepped out to meet those cowboys. The set face and icy voice were reserved for her. He was never again going to be open with her to truly listen to what she had to tell him.

But he was certainly going to *talk* to her, she thought. She would make sure he explained, and in detail, what was happening with Angie and that painting. This change of heart would put her in an embarrassing position with Lucille Kelly, and she was going to know the reason for that no matter how hard it was to communicate with him.

The rest of the day was interminable. Jarod seemed to be near her every minute, no matter what aspect of the celebration she was involved with, and at the same time he seemed as far away as the moon. He was caught up in showing his friends around the inside of the store while she conducted the first raffle drawing of the day, the one for a free pair of boots. When she went back outside to watch Virgil videotape the buggy ride, Jarod came out to see the noisy cowboys off and to put Jesse into one of the buggies.

He stood beside her as the horse clopped away, but he was talking to someone else. While she waited to question him, Angie, Darlene and Billy appeared, along with what seemed to be a dozen other relatives and friends. He was surrounded once more.

Darlene spoke with Sabrina briefly, and Angie gave her an uncertain smile. The girl looked so miserable that Sabrina wanted to reassure her that her decision to keep the painting wasn't the end of the world, but she eluded her, melting into the group and then drifting back inside the store before Sabrina could say anything to her at all.

Lucille Kelly arrived just as Jesse's buggy returned.

"Sabrina!" she trilled, in a voice so like Brenda's that they could have been twins instead of mother and daughter. "How are you, dear? You absolutely look like an Indian princess! What a darling idea!"

Jarod and his family collected Jesse and went back into the store; Lucille and Sabrina followed. "I cannot *wait* to see this painting," Lucille exclaimed. "Nor to meet the artist!"

Sabrina forced her eyes and her thoughts away from Jarod. His broad back seemed to fill the space in front of her.

"Lucille, I'm afraid there's been a bit of a problem," she said smoothly. "The painting won't be available after all."

"What! You haven't let Robbie Spears have it! Sabrina, you promised it to me!"

"No, no," Sabrina soothed, guiding Lucille to the refreshment table, which now held tiny cookies and fresh fruit, along with a variety of cold drinks to combat the heat. "Robbie and her collection have nothing at all to do with this. The artist has simply decided to keep the piece."

While Lucille selected several cookies with her pudgy, beringed fingers, Sabrina involuntarily looked for Jarod again. He was shepherding his group in the direction of his apartment.

She had to get out of here, she thought grimly. She couldn't bear to see him any more today.

She resisted the urge to massage her throbbing temples and fixed her eyes on Lucille again. She would get rid of the woman as soon as she could and then she'd go home and collapse.

"Lucille, I have a couple of other things by this same girl," she said, "and if you like them, I could probably get you one or two more."

Lucille picked up a cup, holding it out to be filled with punch. "I'll take whatever you have."

"You really ought to look at them first," Sabrina suggested. "So far you have nothing but my word for their quality and you may not even like her style."

Lucille demolished a cookie with one determined crunch. "I intend to be the first to own an Angie

Fourkiller painting,'' she announced firmly. "I've already mentioned her to Robbie Spears and a couple of other people."

She sipped daintily at the punch. "That's what scared me. I was afraid that Robbie had rushed down here and somehow talked you out of my painting."

"No," Sabrina reassured her. She regarded the woman thoughtfully. "But I don't know, Lucille. None of the ones I have will fit into your Madonna collection."

"That's all right. I'll simply hang them someplace else. Robbie has lorded it over me for a year because she discovered J. L. Harjo's sculptures. I'm not letting that happen again." She put down her cup. "Now, where are these masterpieces? I want to see what I've just bought."

Sabrina smiled in relief as she led her to the art department. She should have remembered Lucille's single-minded competitiveness. Angie's career was safe.

In spite of Sabrina's efforts to move her toward the door, Lucille wouldn't leave. First she raved about Angie's talent and her new purchases, then thoroughly discussed Robbie and finally repeated all of Brenda's invitations designed to bring Sabrina back into circulation. Sabrina was limp with exhaustion by the time she finally left.

She went back to her office and collected her purse, telling Zelda that she could be reached at home for the next hour or so. Then she drove through the sweltering heat, trying to make her mind a blank, trying to forget that the store would be open until nine in the evening and that she would have to go back there before then.

She opened the massive door of her condominium and stepped in. It swung silently closed behind her; she leaned back against it.

At last she was safe in her private retreat from the world. Here she wouldn't have to deal with Virgil or with Angie or Lucille.

Here she wouldn't have to see Jarod.

Her eyes roamed the massive living area with its wide, curving glass wall and perfectly arranged furnishings. Everything about the white and blue decor was exactly right. Elegant furniture, books and paintings were perfectly arranged in the room's spaciousness. It should be the cool haven she'd been longing for all day.

But it was cold instead. Cold and empty in spite of all the *things* that tried to fill it. Sabrina shivered.

She dropped her purse onto a table and crossed slowly to sink into the deep luxury of the couch, suddenly too drained to go any farther. She crossed her arms in front of her, absently massaging them as if that could warm her.

Maybe Jarod would be gone when she went back to the store, she thought. Maybe she wouldn't have to see him again today.

Of course he would be gone. He'd have some sort of plans to celebrate the success of the big grand opening. Plans that didn't include her.

She stared out across the distant expanse of the city. There had been a time when she'd assumed that she and Jarod would have a victorious celebration together when this important day was over.

Well, then, this was very appropriate, she thought bitterly. After all, nothing in her whole life was turning out according to her dreams.

Chapter Twelve

Jarod pushed open the door to Cowboy's as if it were an enemy and waited for Billy to precede him into the popular night spot.

"Look, Jarod," Billy said over his shoulder as he led the way to a table, "you didn't want to come, you shoulda said somethin'."

"It was my idea, remember?" Jarod growled.

He felt Billy's sharp eyes flick over his face and he made a conscious effort to relax. He'd barely responded to Billy's attempts at conversation during the short drive over from the store; now he was snapping his head off. Pretty rotten treatment for somebody he'd asked out for a drink.

A waitress materialized beside the table and they ordered; as soon as she was gone, he apologized. "I'm sorry, Billy. I'm in a really rank mood. Too much grand opening, I guess."

"Didn't seem to be," Billy disagreed. "Looked like you was havin' a great ol' time there at the store."

"Yeah, well, I'm a great actor, too."

And that was no lie, he thought as he glanced around at the assorted Friday night revelers that filled the place. If he hadn't been a great actor he'd have grabbed Sabrina the minute he saw her all dressed up like an Indian and shaken her until that black hair had been floating in a cloud all around her head. No, he would've kissed her so hard . . .

Billy's eyes followed Jarod's glance. "Ever'body's ready for some honkey-tonkin'," he remarked, raising his voice against the first loud licks played by the fiddler in the six-piece band.

"Yeah."

The waitress appeared, weaving her way through the couples on their way to the dance floor; she served their drinks with a dazzling smile. Everybody was happy tonight, Jarod thought sourly. And he felt like throwing a chair through the window.

The lead guitarist and the mandolin player joined the fiddler, then the drummer, rhythm guitarist and bass man cut into the song in earnest. The tune was an old one, one that had been used to let out pure joy for more years than anybody could remember.

Jarod shifted restlessly and took a big swallow of his drink. They could at least play some sad music.

Billy was tapping his fingers on the table in rhythm with the beat. "Reminds me of the old dances over at Park Hill," he said. "Don't it you?" He smiled. "Danced till sunup nearly every Sunday mornin'."

Jarod nodded. That was a million years ago—before he'd ever come to Tulsa. Before he'd met Diane. Or Sabrina.

Now his nerves were strung so tight around his very bones he felt as if he could never dance again.

He set the glass down and moved it around on the table, watching the little moist circles it made. He could feel Billy watching him, but he didn't look up.

"Well, you got your store open," Billy said, in still another effort at creating a real conversation. "Got it all under control. Customers rollin' in and the Channel 2 sportscaster sayin' last night he's bettin' on you to win the all-around buckle again. Can't ask for more than that, huh?"

Jarod grunted.

"'Cept maybe a woman?" Billy's voice was soft under the music of the band. "One certain woman?"

Jarod's head jerked up. Billy's eyes were understanding. Remembering. Sympathetic.

Jarod felt his mouth twist wryly. He shrugged. "That *is* one thing I *don't* have under control."

Billy took a drink of beer. When he spoke again, his tone was as carefully casual as his question. "How come?"

"It's a hopeless deal," Jarod said in a bitter rush, relief flowing through him at actually putting his misery into words. "It's just another one of my pointless obsessions, Billy. Don't worry about it."

"Why pointless?"

"You said it yourself that time I brought her to your house," Jarod said impatiently. "I ought to be done with that type of woman." He made some more circles with the glass. "And Ray Pigeon said it at the rodeo. With her, I'm way out of my class."

"Some people talk too much."

"Not that time. It's the truth."

"You love her." It was a statement, not a question.

"Yeah."

"She love you?"

"She says she does."

Billy nursed his drink and the thought. "So what're you waitin' for?"

Jarod stared at him. "For her to decide that she wants to live in a log cabin way out in the country. For her to forget about country clubs and society balls. For her to want to spend her life with a man whose career scares her to death. A man who was going down the road while she was going to one of the best colleges in the country." He shrugged contemptuously. "That's all I'm waiting for. That and a blizzard in July."

"All that's real important to her, huh? She say so?"

"No. But one of her old friends was in the store this morning and that's all she was talking about. Lunches, committee meetings, the club." He tossed down another gulp. "Face it, Billy. As soon as she's been back here for a little while she'll be into all that again. And there's no room for me in that kind of a life."

"Just like there wasn't room for you in Diane's when she went off to Europe?"

"Exactly."

"More I see of her she don't seem so much like Diane."

"Well, she is," Jarod snapped.

Billy shook his head. "I'm older and wiser," he said, taking another careful sip from his glass. "I know you like a son. I was watchin' you and her at the store a while ago. You're in a whole lot deeper this time than you ever were with Diane. Better ask her to marry you."

"No." The music stopped as he spoke and the word seemed uncommonly loud.

"If she told you she loved you I doubt she'd say no."

"That's not the problem. I'm scared she'd say yes."

Billy stared at him in silence. The fiddle sounded the beginning of a new song, this time a mournfully sad one.

"I wouldn't be responsible," Jarod declared. "I'm not going to have her unhappiness on my head."

"You can't know she'd be unhappy."

Jarod looked down and swirled the drink in his glass. "She would. She didn't exactly fit right in with the clan that day at your house, did she? She doesn't understand; she can't even communicate with Angie—she's got her all upset. And . . ."

"That's not Sabrina's fault and you know it."

Jarod ignored him. "And she'd have to give up too much to be my wife. Way too much."

Billy was quiet. His black eyes were hard and imperturbable.

"I'm going to talk to her," Jarod said, sounding defensive, even to himself. "But not about marriage. I'll explain about Angie and the painting."

"You better talk about gettin' together, too. Way you've been talkin', I can see this thing is eatin' you up alive."

"No."

Jarod stood up abruptly, scraping the heavy chair across the hardwood floor. He slipped his fingers into the tight back pocket of his jeans and brought out his wallet.

"Come on," he said roughly. "Let's go find a place where they can play something besides this damned old hurting music."

Billy stood up, too, but he didn't move away from the table. His eyes never left Jarod's. "You can't live like this. You two are gonna have to try it, Jarod. You know that."

Jarod threw some bills onto the table in a crumpled heap. "Then she's the one who'll have to come to me."

Sabrina had been at the store for nearly two hours the next morning before she admitted that Jarod wasn't going to show up. She'd thought of nothing but him for most of the night and she had come to work determined to end her misery. She'd make him explain to her about Angie and that painting and after that she'd see him as little as was humanly possible.

She thought of Martin's parting words and smiled bitterly. He might think she could do anything, but she couldn't make Jarod see her love for him. He wasn't going to let her do that. She had no choice but to give up and change the way she looked at him. They were simply two people from different worlds who'd had something good together for a little while.

Restlessly she got up and paced over to her window. She'd watched Jarod leave from here, she thought involuntarily. Only a month or so ago. It might as well have been years. And as far as she was concerned he might as well never have come back.

She turned and went back to her desk, but the horrible scenes of every meeting she'd had with Jarod since his return came flooding into her mind as if a dam had broken. And the sensations of desire he'd aroused in her came with them in spite of her frustration and anger.

She opened a drawer and reached for her purse. She had to get out of here. She wasn't going to spend the rest of the day scurrying from department to department, from her office to the front counter, trying to escape the awful memories of the day before.

She went out into the outer office. "Zelda, I'm going out for a while."

"Well, I hope you're going to see Molly Bear and get another dress," Zelda said firmly. "Your modeling yesterday sold the one I was saving my money for."

"It did?"

"Yes. That phone call a minute ago was from a Mr. Talliaferro. He said that he noticed it on you yesterday and he wants to buy it for his wife."

"Great!"

"It's not great," Zelda disagreed, with a pout. "I never had a chance."

Sabrina smiled. The woman had given her the perfect destination. She'd get away and accomplish something constructive at the same time.

"You have a chance at the next one," she promised. "I'll go straight to Molly's right now and see if she's finished yet."

"But she doesn't know you're coming," Zelda objected. "What about an interpreter?"

"Oh, no! I forgot about that!" Sabrina frowned. She'd gotten along so well with Molly during her first visit that the language barrier had been nothing. But Jarod *had* been interpreting.

She pushed away the memories that threatened her and forced herself to think. "It's Saturday!"

"So?"

"Her sister goes home from her job in Tulsa every weekend. She's the one I talked to on the phone when I made the first appointment. She can interpret."

"Well, I don't care who does the translating, just so Molly understands that she needs to hurry with more dresses," Zelda teased.

"I'll make sure she knows that," Sabrina assured her, laughing. She gave the woman a few instructions, then left the store. As soon as she stepped outside she noticed that clouds had begun covering the sun. It was a wonderful relief from the pitiless sunshine that had been beating down on the city for days, and when she got to her car she let the top down. Driving with the wind in her hair would help clear her mind, she thought. And maybe it'd blow away all the memories of the last time she'd made this trip. She drove very fast out of the parking lot and then up onto the expressway, heading toward Highway 51.

In spite of her hopes to the contrary, every mile of the trip had brought back a different thought of Jarod, and when she bounced over the last stretch of Molly's dirt road and found Ridge sitting on the woman's front porch, she wanted to scream. This wasn't getting away at all. She was getting deeper into the haunting remembrances all the time.

The sound of the car door brought Molly and the woman who was obviously her sister out onto the porch.

Molly beamed and welcomed her with a spate of Cherokee that her sister, who introduced herself as Dalah, translated. "She says it's good you're here. It's no good driving in this weather."

Startled, Sabrina glanced at the sky above the trees that surrounded the little clearing. She'd been so caught up in her thoughts that she'd paid no attention to the weather. The clouds were darkening, she saw, and the wind was stronger, but it certainly didn't seem too bad for traveling.

She nodded her thanks, and returned the greeting.

Dalah started to introduce Sabrina to Ridge, but he waved the words away and greeted her with an unhurried nod. "Sabrina," he pronounced solemnly. He went back to his study of the sky without another word.

"Sit down," Molly invited, through Dalah. "Sit and we'll talk."

Sabrina took the rush-seated rocking chair and the two women settled into the long porch swing.

"Did you have a good trip?" Dalah asked.

"Very nice, thank you."

"Was it stormy in Tulsa?"

"No, it was cloudy, but that's all."

Sabrina started the chair rocking with an impatient motion. She really hadn't come all the way down here to talk about the weather, but she hated to plunge right into business. She knew that the Cherokee considered it impolite to do so.

"We missed you at the grand opening celebration yesterday," she told them. "I wish you could've come."

Molly shook her head and made a brief remark. "Too far," Dalah translated. She smiled at Sabrina. "Molly doesn't like Tulsa," she explained. "She's only been there twice in her life."

"And you work there," Sabrina marveled.

"Yes. I love it."

Molly began what was obviously a response to that, even though Dalah hadn't interpreted the English for her.

Ridge interrupted, saying something rapidly in Cherokee and gesturing toward the southwest. The wind picked up and swirled some of the dirt in the bare yard into a dancing dust devil.

The draft held a force it hadn't possessed before and Sabrina felt it touch her with a strange coolness. A storm might be brewing, after all, she thought. Impolite or not, she really ought to mention the dresses and get on her way back, just in case.

But Dalah was getting up. "I'll see what the television man says. Sabrina, you want to come in and look at Molly's new leaf designs?"

Sabrina followed her into the stimulating riot of color that was Molly's living room. Dalah pointed her to several supple buckskin pouches that covered a low table; each of them bore a different beaded leaf design—large and beautifully simple, infused with a silent love of nature. Sabrina picked one up, then glanced away to look at the screen when the voice of the meteorologist boomed into the room.

"...funnels sighted over Coweta and Fort Gibson," he was saying. "With the strongest being seven miles west-southwest of Tahlequah moving into the north-northwest at twenty miles per hour. If you are caught in the open, do not try to outrun the tornado. Take shelter in a ditch or depression...."

A tremendous clap of thunder interrupted him.

Sabrina stared at the tiny funnel storm warning symbol in the corner of the screen, then at the weather man. He was pointing to a spot on his map that seemed to be very near the area where they were.

"That's us," Dalah confirmed. "It's coming right this way."

She switched off the set and Sabrina followed her back to the porch.

"We'd better go to the cellar," Dalah announced. "The strongest one they've sighted is coming this way."

Ridge and Molly rose and started down the steps. Sabrina hesitated, waiting for Dalah, who was closing the front door. Obviously it was too late to leave now; she'd be trying to drive right into the storm.

Dalah secured the latch and she and Sabrina followed the others around the corner of the house. A blinding streak of lightening split the sky.

At that minute the rain hit, pelting into the dry ground with the force of a pile driver. The drops were huge and far apart, but in a matter of seconds they were falling in concentrated sheets.

Sabrina gasped as the cold rain soaked her back; only then did she realize she was still carrying the soft beaded bag. She tried to wrap it in the folds of her denim skirt and run at the same time. Dalah touched her arm to guide her and they reached the others just as Ridge jerked open the metal door to the cellar that slanted out of the hillside.

Molly went first; she lighted a lantern at the bottom of the steps as Sabrina started down them. She turned back, though, when she heard Ridge grunt.

He was hanging on to the door, unable to pull it closed because of the force of the wind. She stepped up and reached for the edge of it, clinging to it inspite of the sharp edge of the sheet metal pressing into her hand and the freezing water beating onto her face.

Dalah was between them, lending her not inconsiderable weight, and at last they were able to close the door. Within seconds they were all inside and Ridge was hooking the latch against the lash of the rain and the horrifying screech of the wind.

"Come over here and dry yourself off, honey," Dalah told her, hurrying to take a towel from a stack on the folding cot in the corner. "You got yourself soaked trying to close that door."

Dalah disregarded her own discomfort to help Sabrina towel her hair. Molly brought a shawl and wrapped it around her wet back, clucking to herself like a mother hen and muttering Cherokee phrases in a worried tone. Suddenly Sabrina was warmed by more than the dry wool. They really cared about her; it felt marvelous to be fussed over.

"Sabrina, come over here and sit," Ridge said, moving a chair out of the shadows. "We may be here a while."

His tone and the way he looked at her were different from before; the shared adventure seemed to have made them friends. She smiled at him and sank gratefully into the creaky old lawn chair he offered.

As Molly and Dalah dried off and bustled around taking care of the towels and finding wraps, Sabrina inspected her surroundings. The cellar was a miniature home: besides three cots and the linens, it held chairs, more flashlights and lanterns, several tools, some clothes and rows and rows of home-canned food on the crude shelves that covered one wall. It was warmly cozy, but it had the cool smell of deep, damp earth.

"I never did like to go to the cellar," Ridge remarked, pulling a chair up beside hers. "But this time I was glad to get here."

"So was I," Sabrina admitted.

He leaned forward to pull a pipe from his hip pocket, then took a cloth sack of tobacco from his shirt and began fixing a smoke. It seemed as if he were settling in for a nice, long talk. She felt, more than she saw, his eyes on her in the dimness.

"You seen Jarod lately?"

She started, jerking her head toward him, Jarod's name slicing through her.

She swallowed. "Yesterday," she said.

"How is he? I ain't seen him since he went to that last batch of rodeos."

"He's fine."

Molly moved the lantern to a tall box behind Ridge's head. It threw his face into relief; he was watching Sabrina as if he were divining every detail of her last meeting with his grandson.

Dalah and Molly were looking for rags and stuffing them into the leaks around the door, talking softly in Cherokee. Their liquid voices were the only sounds besides the rain and the wind.

Then an enormous clap of thunder obliterated every other noise. Sabrina jumped, startled.

Ridge chuckled. "You're not scared of thunder, are you? You know the Cherokees are called the Friends of Thunder?"

"I didn't know."

He dropped his eyes to the match in his hand. "So my grandson never told you that," he said thoughtfully. He struck the match against the rough concrete floor and lit the pipe. "You ever hear the story of Thunder and the Turtle?"

She smiled and shook her head.

He glanced up sharply.

"No."

"Well, this is the tale the old men told," he said, drawing on the pipe. "One day Thunder and the Turtle were talking. The Turtle asked Thunder to be his fighting partner. So Thunder asked the Turtle, 'What can you do?'

"The Turtle ran and jumped on a twig and broke off a small piece of it. 'That is what I can do,' he said. Then he asked Thunder, 'What can you do?'

" 'I can do this,' said Thunder. He created lightening. It struck a tree and tore it into little splinters.

"The Turtle ran away and went into the water, and that's when he started living in the water. Even today he doesn't come out of it when it rains and thunders. He was scared of Thunder when he splintered the tree and he's been scared ever since."

His sharp eyes flicked to hers, then away. He drew at the pipe.

"Turtle wouldn't try anymore to get to know Thunder and that's why they never became partners."

The soft voice stopped and Sabrina sat, listening to the rain. Listening to the words all over again.

The crashing of the rain against the door and the vent pipes changed abruptly to quick, sharp pinging noises. They grew louder and louder.

"Hail," Ridge said in answer to her startled glance. "Funnel maybe gettin' close."

Sabrina took a long, shaky breath. Oh, dear God, where was Jarod at this very minute? She prayed that he was still in Tulsa. If he happened to be at his cabin . . .

She tried to think. Was there a storm cellar at his place? She couldn't remember seeing one as he'd shown her around.

Even if he had one, he might not be in it. He could have gone to see about the horses. . . .

The memories of the days they'd spent there, isolated in their own sweet world, spun in her head. He had to be all right, she prayed. He couldn't be out in this storm.

The noise of the hail stopped as sharply as it had begun and Sabrina gripped the arms of the chair. She couldn't even breathe. After all that noise, the silence was so oppressive that it seemed to stop time itself.

Then the roar filled it.

"It really does sound just like a freight train," she said, not realizing that the others couldn't possibly hear her.

Then it was gone.

Dalah insisted that they wait for a few minutes, but soon Ridge climbed the steps and pushed open the door. There was no rain, no wind.

Sabrina climbed up behind him into a world that looked as if it had been dropped from another galaxy. A greenish-pink mist was rising everywhere from the hailstones, some of them as big as tennis balls, that littered the ground. She could barely see through it to the trees on the other side of the house.

The house!

Molly emerged from the cellar behind Sabrina and her incoherent cry drowned out Sabrina's gasp of horror. Half the house was gone. The tornado had sliced it neatly down the middle lengthways and had taken the kitchen and one bedroom with it into oblivion. The living room walls were standing, roofless, their bright hangings glowing in the pale sunlight that was already creeping out from behind the clouds.

"What? What is it?" Dalah demanded as she climbed the steps behind them. "Did it hit the house?"

Nobody answered.

She reached the top and came out to stand beside them, her words trailing off into an incoherent moan. They all stood frozen for a long moment, trying to absorb the reality, looking at the hangings on the exposed walls moving in the breeze that now seemed as gentle as spring.

Then Molly and Dalah started toward the house, drawn as if to a lodestone, picking their way through the destruction. Ridge followed at a little distance.

Sabrina couldn't move. She stood at the entrance to the cellar, shivering as the cool air penetrated her wet clothing, unable to force her gaze away from the two women. Her throat tightened with pain. She was hurting with them as they helped each other over the rubble into what was left of their home. They had so little to begin with, she thought, and now half of that was gone and the other half was ruined.

And Molly's work! All those hours of hard work and creative effort completely obliterated in a few seconds time!

A car horn blared, and then she heard the motor. It seemed incredible so soon after the storm's passing but a battered pickup truck was topping the last rise of the rocky road. It roared down into the yard and its occupants piled out with cries of "Are you all right? Anybody hurt?"

Molly and Dalah turned to them with smiles and tears and answering calls of "How'd you get here so fast?"

"It wasn't easy," the driver called back. "We had to come the back way. We heard there's a big pine down across the road just this side of the highway."

There were hugs all around and rejoicing that everyone was alive and well. Dalah and Molly called to Sabrina and she walked slowly toward them, finding herself drawn into the circle and into helping to recount the whole experience.

Within minutes more vehicles arrived, and soon the place was swarming with friends and relatives. They fanned out over the yard and pasture and into the trees, searching for things to salvage.

Sabrina watched for only a few seconds before she rolled up the sleeves of her Western shirt, tied back her still wet hair with the bandana from around her neck and waded into the mess with the others. It might rain again, she thought, as she picked up her skirt to climb over the twisted remains of the front porch. They needed to save all they could.

She worked for almost an hour, getting even wetter and grimier in the process, trying not to wonder whether Jarod's cabin also looked like this. She couldn't get there if she tried; the road was blocked and she didn't know the back way. Of course, she'd find the way if she knew for sure he was there. No, she admitted finally, she'd find the way to him in spite of any obstacles if she knew that he wanted her there.

But she knew he didn't want her there. He'd made that abundantly clear more times than one. They were employer and employee now; like Thunder and the Turtle, they would never become partners.

She paused in taking one of Molly's hangings from the wall, staring at it without seeing it at all. *That* was the reason Ridge had told her the story—he had been divining the problems between her and his grandson!

She looked around for him, smiling to herself. What an old matchmaker he was!

Then the smile faded and she tried to concentrate on folding the hanging to stack with the others. Matchmaker or no, she and Jarod would never get together. They were just as different as Thunder and the Tur-

tle; just as afraid of each other. And their story would
end in the very same way.

She walked to the couch and put the last hanging
carefully on top of the others, forcing herself to think
about what she was doing, willing those thoughts to
blot out the ones of Jarod. What else could she do?
Was there anymore of Molly's work that could be
saved?

The purse! The one she'd carried to the cellar. It was
probably the only piece that wasn't wet or damaged!

She moved back through the wreckage of the porch
and circled out to a relatively clear path. Another vehicle arrived, but she didn't glance behind her as she
bent to pull a battered kitchen chair out of her way.
She'd get the purse and then try to find a garbage bag
or something to wrap all the buckskin in.

But just before she reached the cellar door, she
spotted the little bag caught on a sharp spike of twisted
bedspring, its fringes waving sadly in the wind. The
storm had impaled it through both layers of the
leather; it was torn and spotted by the rain.

Suddenly, irrationally, tears sprang into her eyes,
she put her hands over her face. Even that one last
thing was ruined. She hadn't saved it after all; she
must have dropped it when they were struggling to
close the door.

"Sabrina?"

His voice was harsh with shocked surprise, but even
so its low richness soaked into her consciousness and
through her like a warm, fragrant bath. It set free the

tears of her despair; they were rolling freely down her cheeks when she turned around and looked up into Jarod's dark eyes.

Chapter Thirteen

What's wrong? Sabrina, what are you doing here? Were you hurt in the storm?''

His arms went around her and she let him gather her to him, huddling there as if he were the only haven in the world. The warmth of his nearness was the only comfort she needed.

She tried to bury her face in his chest, but he wouldn't let her.

"Answer me," he demanded, holding her away so he could see her. "Are you all right?"

She nodded. "Yes." She choked on the word and he drew her closer again. She felt him tremble.

"I had no idea you were here," he said into her hair. "If I'd known..."

His arms tightened around her. "Dear God," he breathed, and the words were a prayer. "Sabrina, you could've been killed."

She raised her head, but she slid her arms around him to hold him there. "So could you," she said unsteadily. "Somehow I knew you weren't still in Tulsa."

"No, I . . ." His face darkened and he let the sentence drop.

She moved a little away from him. She didn't want to talk about why he'd suddenly driven away from Tulsa. Nor why she had done so. Not now.

"I was in Tahlequah," he said. "I heard that it hit out here and I rushed to Ridge's place. I had a hell of a time; I had to go the back way. . . ."

"I know. There's a tree across the road."

He raised an eyebrow. "Well, you sound like you know your way around the woods. I thought you were a city girl."

"Not today." She kept her voice from trembling but a shiver went through her body. He was teasing, yet he was still labeling her. She was a fool to be letting him hold her like this.

She tried to step back, but he tightened his arms. "Jarod . . ."

"Jarod!" a loud voice echoed her. "Hey, man, how about givin' us a hand with this thing?"

They turned toward the house. A group of men were clearing a path between the living room furniture and a waiting pickup truck; a heavy roof beam was blocking their way.

"Let me go help them," Jarod said. "Then I want to talk to you."

Her heart leaped into her throat. Had his sudden fear changed his mind about her?

She watched him stride away from her, trying to steel herself against the sensuous appeal of his powerful walk. He might not have meant that at all.

She tried to go back to her salvage of the artwork, but she couldn't keep her eyes away from Jarod. Moving the beam turned out to be a bigger project than anyone had thought, and finally, in spite of the chill still in the air from the melting hail stones, he stripped off his sweat-soaked shirt.

She watched the play of his muscles under his copper-colored skin, fighting the surge of desire they created in her. Her hands could remember exactly the way they felt underneath her palms; her lips could recall the exact taste of his skin.

He pulled the end of the beam up and out of the way at last, using the leverage of his long horseman's legs to heave it far enough from the path. Then he turned and his eyes found hers.

They moved over her with the same slow observation that she'd been giving him, telling her plainly that he'd felt her watching him. They stopped for a leisurely, tingling moment on her breasts. She felt them thrill to him, straining at her rain-dampened shirt.

Then they moved back to her face. They blazed into hers, touching her with fire across the space between them. He still wanted her, they said imperiously. He'd never stopped wanting her.

And she still wanted him, she answered without making a sound.

They stood motionless, tortured by the distance that separated them. Finally somebody called to him and he tore his eyes away.

When she could move again she went to look for a bag to hold the folded buckskin hangings. Her hands trembled with every motion as she took one from the closet of the remaining bedroom.

That deliberating desire had flamed between them the moment they'd met, she thought helplessly, taking the bag back to the living room. Even the awful weeks just past hadn't been able to destroy it.

She slid the hangings into the bag, then loaded it into the truck that Molly indicated. She tried to keep her eyes away from Jarod as she worked, but she was as aware of every movement he made as if she'd been born with antennae just for him.

They found more items to be salvaged under the beam, so he continued to work with the other men and Sabrina helped carry out the clothes on hangers and the bedding. In the middle of that, Dalah came to her to say that Molly was packing the contents of the huge handcarved cabinet that held her beads and leather; she wanted Sabrina to help.

By late afternoon they'd done all they could. Everything that was undamaged was loaded onto various vehicles and Molly and Dalah were set to go stay with relatives.

Jarod came straight to Sabrina. His shirt was hanging loose, open on his chest; beads of sweat stood on his forehead and on his upper lip. She tightened her hands by her sides to keep from reaching up and wiping it away.

"Get your car and follow me. I'll drop Ridge off and then go on to my place," he said gruffly. "You need to get out of those wet clothes."

That phrase brought back a flash of memory that was brilliantly clear against the more recent one of the naked look they'd shared. It recreated the first time they'd made love—that wild, carefree day they'd played in the river—with a force that took the last ounce of her strength.

Well, she couldn't go to his house and make love with him today, she thought, as she watched him and Ridge climbing into his truck. No matter how much they still wanted each other. She could never survive that experience again unless...unless she knew that he loved her.

Sabrina, you could've been killed. The desperate concern with which he'd spoken those words echoed through her. Maybe he *did*....

She wouldn't let herself finish the thought. Quickly she went to find Molly and Dalah and told them goodbye, then she got into her car. In a strange way she was sorry for this experience to end, she thought as she started the motor. She'd been a part of a real community for a while, and she loved it.

She pulled out onto the rutted road after Jarod's truck. She was following him instead of heading back to Tulsa because at last he wanted to talk, she told herself. She'd listen to him; that was all.

At Ridge's place she stopped behind the pickup and he turned to give her a little salute and a nod before he went into the house. She smiled and waved back at him. They were friends now, she realized intuitively. They'd gone through a storm together and he'd told her a story—in some mysterious way that had made them friends. She'd have to come back and see him sometimes even if...

She jerked her mind away from that line of thinking and put the car back into gear to follow Jarod.

The sun was hinting at going down by the time they reached his cabin. He got out of the truck and came around to open her door; she stepped out into the darkening evening. She shivered as the wind coming over the hilltop hit her and went straight through her clothes. "It must've dropped forty degrees since the storm came through," he said. "You go on and get into the shower. I'll be in in a minute."

She hesitated, her arms wrapped around herself in unconscious defense. "But I'm nearly dry, now. You're the one who's wet; you'll catch your death of cold."

"Go on," he urged, taking her shoulders and turning her toward the house. "I won't be long."

She hurried with the shower, trying not to think about those mindlessly content days she'd spent with him in this house. She'd listen to what he had to say, she decided, and after that she could let herself think.

She searched his closet without finding a robe, so she finally decided on a long-tailed flannel cowboy shirt that came halfway to her knees and some of his boot socks. She rolled up the too long sleeves, gathered her filthy, still-damp clothes and took them out to the utility room. She started them washing, then went into the kitchen to heat water for coffee.

The door blew open with a gust of wind and Jarod came in, his arms full of short logs. "Only in Oklahoma," he remarked. "Nowhere else can you be running your air-conditioner at daylight one morning and building a fire in the fireplace that night."

She laughed. "I believe there was a famous Cherokee named Will Rogers who once said something like that."

"Very good," he approved as he carried the wood through to the living room. "I didn't know you knew that he was a Cherokee."

"I'm learning a lot about Cherokees," she called after him. "You'd be surprised at the things I know."

"Like what?" he yelled back.

She walked to the door to look at him. He was squatting on his haunches in front of the fireplace, arranging the logs, taking tinder and kindling from the basket on the hearth. The worn, wet denim of his jeans was straining over the powerful muscles of his thighs; his chest was showing broad and hard where his shirt hung open. She couldn't stand it, she thought. She couldn't stand to be here with him and not cross the room to touch him.

"I'll tell you later," she said, trying to keep her voice even. "You've got to get your shower before we can have supper."

"Supper? Great! You're cooking supper?"

"*We're* cooking supper. It's an old Italian custom for everyone to help in the kitchen."

He laughed as he struck a match and held it to the tinder. "I doubt that! Now that you've learned all about the Cherokees maybe you should do some research on the Italians. You seem to be a little rusty there."

She laughed, too, but instead of continuing the joking, she turned and went back into the kitchen. It was too much like the first time she'd been with him. It was too easy to believe that there were no differences standing between them, nothing to prevent them from being together forever.

When he came out of the shower smelling of soap, his copper skin glowing, she already had the butter hot in the pan and the bread sliced and ready to go into the oven.

"I'm sorry the bread's still frozen," she said, trying desperately to keep from brushing against him as he came to the counter to help her. "I couldn't find any that wasn't."

If she felt his body against hers right now she would turn and go into his arms, no matter how determined she was to resist.

"I forgot bread on my way in last night," he was saying. "My mind was on something else and somehow I only managed to get milk and eggs."

Was that "something else" the two of them? Was it the same impossible maze that had kept her awake for hours? Her hand trembled as she poured the beaten eggs into the pan.

"Let me check on the fire while those cook," he said. "We can eat in there."

When the omelets were done, they carried their plates to the living room and settled onto the rug in front of the hearth, holding the frozen bread to the fire on long forks to be toasted.

"This is delicious," he said as they ate ravenously. "See, it really was best that I didn't help you."

She shook her head, laughing. "No. Next time..."

She stopped. What was she letting this do to her? There might never be a next time.

"Next time I'll help," he promised with a grin. Then he sobered as he finished the last bite of toast and set his plate aside. "Sabrina," he said, "I wanted to talk with you about Angie."

Her hand froze with her coffee mug to her mouth. Angie! Was *that* what he'd wanted to talk to her about?

"I'm sorry she caused you a problem about the painting," he said. "And I'm sorry I jumped all over you about it. She rode back down here with me last night, and for the first time she told me that you already had it promised to someone."

She stared at him. Her arm felt too stiff to set the cup down, but she had to do something with it.

"It's all right," she said finally. "I managed to keep the customer."

Very carefully, she set the mug on the floor. "Look, Jarod, what *is* going on with Angie, anyway?"

"She never intended to sell the painting," he said. "It's one of her most precious possessions because she used her older sister, Rayna, and her little boy, Jesse, to model for it. Rayna died before Jesse was a year old."

Sabrina stared at him, trying to comprehend what he'd just said.

"I thought Jesse was Darlene's."

"He's her grandchild."

"But, Jarod! You said Angie *never* intended to sell the painting? Not from the very first? Then why would she tell me..."

"She's just a little country girl," he interrupted softly. "You're a beautiful, sophisticated lady who appeared out of nowhere at a powwow and started praising her talents. She wanted to please you, to make you happy."

"But deceiving me wouldn't make me happy!"

"She didn't see it as deceiving you. She was hoping that things would never come to the point that she would have to actually refuse to let you have the painting. She thought that you'd forget about it or she could let you have a different painting instead."

She shook her head, amazed. "Poor child! I must have been making her miserable and I didn't even know it. I can't believe she was too afraid to tell me the truth."

"Well, you certainly didn't mean to make her feel that way." He reached for her hand and took it into both of his. She drew a deep, trembling breath.

"And I thought it was the white man who's supposed to speak with forked tongue," she teased, a bit unsteadily.

"White men and Indians are all just people," he said quietly.

"And we shouldn't be afraid of each other?" she ventured.

He smiled and twined her fingers into his. "There's an old Cherokee story about that...."

"Thunder and the Turtle?"

His eyes widened. "You know that story?"

She smiled smugly. "I told you you'd be surprised at all the Cherokee lore I know."

"Where'd you hear it?"

"Your granddad told it to me in the cellar."

He sat very still, the warmth of his palm pulsing into hers.

"I'm not really sure whether I've been Thunder or the Turtle," he said slowly, his eyes fixed on hers. "But somehow, Sabrina, I think that story is about us."

Her heart bounded into her throat and for a long moment she thought it had stopped beating.

He held her hand even more tightly and reached with his other one to cup her cheek and bring her face close to his. "I love you, Sabrina. I can't wait another minute to say that. I've wanted to tell you for so long—I guess for as long as I've known you."

"Then why didn't you?"

"Because I was afraid. Afraid I'd ask you to marry me."

"Would that be so terrible?"

The words were tantalizingly soft, her lips near his, bewitching him. He turned his head and looked into the fire.

"Would it?"

He answered her gentle persistence by speaking to the dancing flames. "The last thing in this world you need is a cowboy for a husband."

"Jarod."

He turned back to her.

"The *only* thing in this world that I need is you for a husband. Whether you're a cowboy or a clothier or a . . . coal miner, I need *you*."

He shook his head doubtfully. "You need a lot of other things, too. I heard you talking to your old friend on opening day. Sabrina, you're accustomed to a kind of life that I don't want and can't lead no matter how much I love you. And I won't ask you to give that up."

"I gave up the kind of life Brenda was talking about long before I met you, Jarod. If you were listening to us, then you heard what she said about my career. She's happy with her life—it's the kind of life you imagine that I want—but *I* want a lot more than that."

"But you don't want a cowboy. Not on a permanent basis. You said you were paralyzed with fear when you saw me ride."

"I was. But you'll be off the circuit soon."

"But I'll never stop riding rough stock. Not until I'm too old to step onto a bronc or a bull. That's just part of me, Sabrina, and I can't change."

"I don't want you to change." She touched his face. "I'll be terrified every time you ride, but I can live with that. I can cope with anything as long as I can live with you."

She traced his cheekbone with her finger. "I love you just the way you are, Jarod. That's what I've been trying to tell you."

"But if I don't change, you'll have to. You'll have to give up an awful lot for us to live together."

She shook her head, smiling into the worry clouding his eyes. "I'll give up a few things and I'll add a few others to your life. Things you've never known you needed before."

He groaned. "Like going to the famous Arrowhead Country Club? How many times a year would I have to show up there?"

She tilted her head to the side, pretending to think. Her eyes flashed back to his. "Twice."

He shook his head ruefully. "I don't know," he teased. "I might be able to manage that."

"I promise to make it as painless as possible."

He smiled, then sobered. "But, Sabrina, darling, I can't move to Tulsa and live in a place like yours. I couldn't spend that kind of money when I have people in my family who can barely buy groceries."

She nodded. "I don't care, Jarod. The apartment's been cold and lonely, anyway. We can sell it and find another place for when we're in town."

"And stay here the rest of the time." It was a flat statement.

"Yes, I love this cabin."

He put her hand to his face. "It's the only home I've had since I left Ridge's when I was thirteen. It's something I have to have." He smiled and shook his head. "But you in a log cabin...I don't know..."

"I've learned a lot," she said stoutly. "I've never been the spoiled rich girl you said I was, and I'm even further from that now."

His grin warmed her to her toes. "I know. I saw you at Molly's, spreading clothes on the fence to dry and picking dishes out of the rubble. You looked like a member of the clan."

She dropped her eyes to the rug and stroked the soft sheepskin. "I wish I could be," she said sadly. "Jarod, I'm still not sure about your family. Do you think they'll ever really accept me?"

He nodded once, very sure. "You're on your way. Why, I'd bet old Jet Magic—and he's the best horse that I've got in that pasture—that you're already in. There's not a soul scattered through these hills right now that hasn't already heard about how you pitched to help at Molly and Dalah's."

"The famous party line at work, huh?"

He grinned. "You got it."

"I want to be in the clan," she said softly. "I really need that. I've never seen or felt such a spirit of community as the one over there this afternoon."

"Yeah," he said thoughtfully. "You get used to living with that and it's hard to do without it."

She sobered. "I don't know, though, Jarod. One thing I can't do without is my work. I can't stay down here so much that I lose my career."

He squeezed her hand. "I'll make you a deal. I'll learn enough to really be your partner at the store if you'll be mine in the horse-breeding business."

"Compromise and partnership all the way?"

"All the way."

"So we're one up on the Thunder and the Turtle?"

"Um-hmm." The word was so low in his throat it was a caress. His eyes were clinging to her face, melting with love for her. "Those two don't know what living is."

Pure happiness was burgeoning inside her, expanding like the growing flames of the fire. It was almost more than she could bear.

It was going to be all right. The words sang in her head. At last, everything was going to be all right.

He cupped her face in both his hands and kissed her once, very lightly, on the lips. She thrilled to him, her eyes searching his.

His hands moved over her shoulders, her arms, onto her bare legs. He watched their progress, absorbing every facet of the way she looked in the glow of the fire.

"I meant to tell you I'm sorry I called you a spoiled rich girl," he said finally, his eyes glinting with mischief. "I knew I was wrong the minute I saw you in this outfit."

She smiled with lazy confidence. "Do you like it? It's all I could find. I looked for your breechclout and feathers, but they must've been hidden somewhere."

"They wouldn't have fit you, anyway," he whispered, his hands sliding up under the long tail of the shirt she was wearing. "This looks great on you."

She reached one hand to draw seductive circles around his ear. "I'm so glad you like it."

"And I *love* you," he growled. "Sabrina, I love you. I want to marry you and live with you and take care of you. Are you sure that's what you want?"

"I've never been so sure of anything in all my life."

His eyes searched hers. The impishness in them faded into wonder and then into pure wanting.

Her breath caught in her throat. She tried to speak, but she could manage only a hoarse whisper. "Kiss me, Jarod...."

He took her into his arms then, with a fierceness that made her tremble. Their mouths met in ravening hunger and they sank into the softness of the rug. There they spent the spell-weaving hours of the night stoking the flames of desire that burned hotter inside them than the red and yellow ones of the fire.

OFFICIAL SWEEPSTAKES INFORMATION

1. **NO PURCHASE NECESSARY.** To enter, complete the official entry/ order form. Be sure to indicate whether or not you wish to take advantage of our subscription offer.

2. Entry blanks have been pre-selected for the prizes offered. Your response will be checked to see if you are a winner. In the event that these are not claimed, a random drawing will be held from all entries received to award not less than $150,000 in prizes. This is in addition to any free, surprise or mystery gifts which might be offered. Versions of this sweepstakes with different prizes will appear in Torstar Ltd. mailings and their affiliates. Winners selected will receive the prize offered in their sweepstakes insert.

3. This promotion is being conducted under the supervision of Marden-Kane, an independent judging organization. By entering the sweepstakes, each entrant accepts and agrees to be bound by these rules and the decisions of the judges which shall be final and binding. Odds of winning in the random drawing are dependent upon the total number of entries received. Taxes, if any, are the sole responsibility of the prize winners. Prizes are non-transferable. All entries must be received by August 31, 1986.

4. This sweepstakes package offers:

1, Grand Prize	: Cruise around the world on the QEII	$100,000 total value
4, First Prizes	: Set of matching pearl necklace and earrings	$ 20,000 total value
10, Second Prizes	: Romantic Weekend in Bermuda	$ 15,000 total value
25, Third Prizes	: Designer Luggage	$ 10,000 total value
200, Fourth Prizes	: $25 Gift Certificate	$ 5,000 total value
		$150,000

Winners may elect to receive the cash equivalent for the prizes offered.

5. This offer is open to residents of the U.S. and Canada, 18 years and older, except employees of Torstar Ltd., its affiliates, subsidiaries, Marden-Kane and all other agencies and persons connected with conducting this sweepstakes. All Federal, State and local laws apply. Void in the province of Quebec and wherever prohibited or restricted by law. Winners will be notified by mail and may be required to execute an affidavit of eligibility and release which must be returned within 14 days after notification. Canadian winners will be required to answer a skill testing question. Winners consent to the use of their names, photograph and/or likeness for advertising and publicity purposes in conjunction with this and similar promotions without additional compensation. One prize per family or household.

6. For a list of our most current prize winners, send a stamped, self-addressed envelope to: WINNERS LIST, c/o Marden-Kane, P.O. Box 10404, Long Island City, New York 11101.

SSR-A-1

Silhouette Special Edition

COMING NEXT MONTH

NOBODY'S FOOL—Renee Roszel
Cara never minded a little fun and games . . . but only on her own terms. So when businessman Martin Dante challenged her to a nine-mile race, she feared the results would be "winner take all!"

THE SECURITY MAN—Dixie Browning
Though Valentine had survived both a bad marriage and an accident that had left her widowed, she wasn't quite ready for her new handsome neighbor. Val couldn't risk loving, but with Cody it was all too tempting.

YESTERDAY'S LIES—Lisa Jackson
Iron willed and proud, Tory was not about to be manipulated, especially not by Trask McFadden. The attractive young senator had deceived her in the past—could he convince her that this time his love was real?

AFTER DARK—Elaine Camp
Sebastian was a man haunted by the past. Everly was a woman determined to control her future. Now he was back to reclaim her heart. Could she be convinced of the healing power of love?

MAGIC SEASON—Anne Lacey
Independence was her trademark and Game Warden Laura Marchand kept her image with spit and polish. But sportsman Ryan D'Arco was hunting her territory and was about to capture her heart.

LESSONS LEARNED—Nora Roberts
Juliet could smell success when she was assigned to do the publicity tour for Italy's most famous chef. But Carlo distracted her with his charms, setting his romantic recipes simmering in her heart.

AVAILABLE NOW:

AMERICAN TRIBUTE

Where a man's dreams count
for more than his parentage...

*Look for these upcoming titles
under the Special Edition
American Tribute banner.*

CHEROKEE FIRE
Gena Dalton #307—May 1986
It was Sabrina Dante's silver spoon that
Cherokee cowboy Jarod Redfeather couldn't
trust. The two lovers came from opposite
worlds, but Jarod's Indian heritage taught
them to overcome their differences.

NOBODY'S FOOL
Renee Roszel #313—June 1986
Everyone bet that Martin Dante and Cara
Torrence would get together. But Martin
wasn't putting any money down, and Cara
was out to prove that she was nobody's fool.

MISTY MORNINGS, MAGIC NIGHTS
Ada Steward #319—July 1986
The last thing Carole Stockton wanted was to
fall in love with another politician, especially
Donnelly Wakefield. But under a blanket of
secrecy, far from the campaign spotlights,
their love became a powerful force.

AM-TRIB-1R

Silhouette Special Edition

AMERICAN TRIBUTE

*American Tribute titles
now available:*

RIGHT BEHIND THE RAIN
Elaine Camp #301—April 1986
The difficulty of coping with her brother's
death brought reporter Raleigh Torrence
to the office of Evan Younger, a police
psychologist. He helped her to deal with
her feelings and emotions, including love.

THIS LONG WINTER PAST
Jeanne Stephens #295—March 1986
Detective Cody Wakefield checked out
Assistant District Attorney Liann McDowell,
but only in his leisure time. For it was the
danger of Cody's job that caused Liann to
shy away.

LOVE'S HAUNTING REFRAIN
Ada Steward #289—February 1986
For thirty years a deep dark secret kept them
apart—King Stockton made his millions while
his wife, Amelia, held everything together.
Now could they tell their secret, could they
admit their love?